Midwinter Magic

A Rockliffe Christmas Novella

Stella Riley

CONTENTS

Prologue
Sarre Park, 1778, three weeks before Christmas …

'Oh. That's a shame,' murmured Caroline, frowning at the letter in her hand. 'Nell and Harry won't be coming after all.'

'They won't?' Looking up from his own correspondence, Adrian reached for the coffee-pot. 'Why not?'

'With a great many apologies, crossings-out and exclamation marks, Nell says that Harry's older brother has summoned them to Wiltshire. Apparently, this is unheard of because he's virtually a recluse – so Harry is naturally worried about what may be behind it.'

'As well he might be. Harry is about as anxious to be a marquis as Nicholas is to be a duke. However, regarding the house-party … do we have final numbers yet?'

'I think so. As we expected, Aristide won't leave Sinclairs over Christmas. And both the Ingrams and the Vernons have declined because their infants are too young to either travel or be left in the care of nurse-maids.'

'Leaving us with Rock and Adeline, Nick and Madeleine, the Amberleys and … who else?'

'The Audleys, the Chalfonts, Lily Brassington and, weather permitting, my grandfather.'

Adrian's brows rose. 'Presumably Julian and Arabella will bring the children?'

'Of course,' grinned Caroline. 'Aside from the fact this will be their first Christmas as a family, you don't think I was going to lose the chance of having a tame virtuoso in the house throughout Yule by *not* inviting them, do you?'

'Ah. You intend to make the poor fellow sing – or rather *play* – for his supper?'

'According to Arabella, he doesn't take much forcing. But seriously … Benedict will be sharing the nursery with Rosalind's two as well as

Vanessa Jane … so three older children will be no trouble at all.' She eyed him thoughtfully. 'Are you *sure* you don't wish to invite your mother?'

'As sure as *you* are about not inviting yours.'

'There's a difference. The dowager would almost certainly refuse. Mama wouldn't.'

'Yes. There is that, I suppose.'

'There is. And I'd spend all of Christmas on a knife-edge, wondering what she'll do or say next,' said Caroline. 'I've never forgotten the look on Marcus Sheringham's face when she asked him what sort of lord he was.'

Adrian gave a crack of laughter. 'She didn't!'

'She did – and then didn't hide the fact that she'd been hoping for something better than a mere baron. Yes, I know it's funny *now*. But it won't be when she says something similar to Nicholas or Sebastian. Also, she and Grandpapa Maitland do not get on with each other. And finally, if Lavinia and Sylvia came as well as Mama, we'd need another two bedchambers.'

'In addition to the twenty we already have?'

'Since half of those are in the south wing, yes.' She eyed him with a touch of exasperation. 'Adrian … I know you leave household matters entirely in my hands but surely you must have noticed that since the north wing was renovated, I've spent the last year decorating and furnishing it? And that two pairs of bedchambers have been combined into suites?'

'Yes, of course,' he replied, uneasily aware that he was missing something.

'So presumably you've *also* realised that, aside from stripping out horrid old mattresses and moth-eaten hangings, nothing has been touched in the *south* wing – and won't be until I'm ready to make similar improvements there?'

'Oh. No. I hadn't … that hadn't actually occurred to me.'

'Clearly,' returned Caroline sardonically. 'The Ingrams and the Vernons declined their invitations weeks ago – which meant everyone can be accommodated in the north wing, and the south left shabby and half-furnished.'

'So the only spare bedchamber fit for occupation is the one reserved for Harry and Nell? Yes. I see. '

'Finally!' she muttered.

'So ... no Hayward ladies?' he asked meekly.

'No. And stop trying to look disappointed, you fraud. I know what you're thinking.'

Adrian laughed. 'I sincerely hope not. However ... just your grandfather. And friends.'

She nodded, suddenly bright with anticipation.

'It will be fun, won't it? There'll be parlour games and kissing boughs ... and the wassailers on Christmas Eve. Perhaps we might hold a ball and invite all the neighbouring families. What do you think?'

He reached across the table to take her hand.

'If you want a ball, sweetheart – and will save at least one dance for me – then a ball you shall have.'

'Thank you. As for other sorts of entertainment, Bertrand has some ideas and --'

'I'll bet he has.'

'And he's volunteered to organise them.'

A look of alarm crossed Adrian's face before melting into mild hilarity.

'God help us,' he said.

Sarre Park, ten days before Christmas ...

CHAPTER ONE

On the day before most of her guests were due to arrive, the Countess of Sarre and her housekeeper toured every corner of the house, checking (for the fifth time) that everything was in readiness. As on the previous four occasions, they found that it was. Windows sparkled, floors and furniture gleamed and bedchambers glowed with new, costly hangings; fires burned in every room to drive out the December chill and the hall was decked with festive greenery.

'Doesn't it look lovely, Betsy?' demanded Caroline, delighted with her efforts.

'Very nice.' Mrs Holt's tone was guarded.

Deliberately ignoring this lack of enthusiasm, Caroline said uncertainly, 'We *have* thought of everything, haven't we?'

'We thought of everything before the invitations went out, my lady – and everything we thought of has been done, along with a good deal else.'

'Yes. I daresay you're right but --'

'I *am* right, my lady. And the summer party went off without a hitch, didn't it?'

'The August party was smaller. Twelve adults and six children this time – not to mention nursery maids, ladies' maids and valets! And I've no idea how we're going to accommodate all the carriages.'

'Mr Didier's seeing to that – making sure our stables are ready to cope as well as the ones at Devereux House in case they should be needed,' said Mrs Holt. And consulting her list of notes, 'Now ... you can leave it to Mr Croft and me to get everyone settled when they arrive – Lord and Lady Amberley are to have the same suite as last time so her ladyship will find her way about alright. Cook is aware that the duchess, Lady Nicholas and Mistress Audley are increasing and may have odd fancies. So far as I can see, there's not a thing left to do except put some seasonal whatnot in the dining and drawing rooms – but that must wait till Christmas Eve. Say what you will, my lady, but none of this,' she gestured to the festoons of holly, ivy and pine decorating the hall, 'ought to be in the house yet.'

'I realise that's the usual tradition,' said Caroline patiently. 'But when the children arrive – most particularly Lord Chalfont's wards – I want them to walk into the house and know right away that Christmas is special.'

'And that's a kind thought, my lady. But it'll still bring bad luck – you mark my words.'

'I marked them the first time you said them, Betsy – and I don't agree. Why *should* it bring ill luck? No reason at all. It's just an old wives' tale.'

'Well, maybe it is and maybe it isn't,' came the stubborn reply. 'But I reckon his lordship was in the right when he said there was to be no more of it till the proper time.'

'He didn't say that because he's superstitious. He said it because he thinks the gentlemen and older children will enjoy going out to cut fresh boughs and everyone will have fun decorating the house with them.' Caroline chuckled and deftly changed the subject. 'Personally, I can't imagine Rockliffe tramping about in the damp and wind, hacking down bits of holly ... but I expect Adrian knows best. Where is he, by the way? I haven't seen him since breakfast.'

'No. You wouldn't have, my lady.' Mrs Holt sniffed. 'He went out riding with Mr Didier three hours ago before either of them could be asked to do anything useful. I doubt we'll see hide nor hair of them till dinner – though I suppose that's better than having the pair of them underfoot, getting in everybody's way.'

* * *

Having completed a couple of small errands, the two errant gentlemen sat by the hearth of the Old New Inn in Sandwich holding tankards of ale and waiting for slices of game pie to sustain them through the afternoon. Not for the first time, conversation had ground to a halt. Adrian let the silence linger for a few minutes and then, sighing, said, 'For God's sake, Bertrand – get over it, can't you? We both knew these changes had to be made and goodness knows it's taken me long enough to get around to them.'

'You could have gone *on* not getting around to them.'

'No. I couldn't. You are not and never have been my bloody servant – and I won't have you continuing to behave as if you were.'

'That's not what I was doing,' muttered Bertrand.

'Oh, I'll give you that. *You* were playing an annoying and over-familiar fellow, like the barber in Beaumarchais' play– which fortunately I don't mind and Caroline finds entertaining. But you can't do that forever.'

'Why not? I was happy doing it. I had a function. And now, with your damned butler and your idiot valet, I don't.'

Adrian drew a long, sustaining breath while the maid set down two steaming portions of pie. He nodded his thanks to her and, when she moved away, said quietly, 'You are my friend and my son's godfather. Isn't that enough?'

'I don't need to live in your house for that.' Bertrand pushed his tankard aside and prodded the pie. 'Perhaps it's time I left.'

'And go where? To do what?'

'London? Maybe Aristide can find work for me at Sinclairs.'

'I daresay he would – if that's what you want. Is it?'

The reply was a surly shrug.

Repressing another sigh, Adrian reflected that, though he didn't do it often, no one could sulk as successfully as Bertrand. He said, 'Are you going to keep this up throughout Yule? Because if so, I'm likely to have throttled you before Twelfth Night.'

For the first time, a gleam of amusement appeared in the Frenchman's eyes.

'Don't worry. I'll play the clown in public, same as always.'

'And snarl at me in private? Well, I suppose that's a relief of sorts.' Adrian cut a piece of pie and ate it. Finally he said, 'Here's an idea. If it's a job you want, take over management of Devereux House and its land. I've more than enough to keep me busy, dealing with Sarre Park. And before you point out that the house belongs to Benedict, try recalling that it's going to be a couple of decades at least before he'll want it. If you're sick of living with Caroline and me --'

'That isn't it at all.'

'It's what it sounds like. So go and live on the bay – have your own establishment, by all means. But do not talk to me about going off to God knows where. And particularly don't talk about it *now* when the house is going to be full of guests and Caroline is depending on you to help with the entertainments.' Adrian grinned suddenly. '*She's* calling you the Master of Ceremonies. You and *I* know you're more likely to be the Lord of Misrule.'

* * *

Carriages began rolling up the drive on the following afternoon. First to arrive, since they came from the shortest distance, was the Wynstanton Priors party. Not only the duke and duchess with their daughter ... but also Lord and Lady Nicholas. The gentlemen had elected to ride but, thanks to maids, valets and luggage, the party still occupied three carriages.

Shaking hands with Bertrand, Rockliffe murmured, 'On the assumption you will be struggling for space, I have instructed my fellows to take two of the carriages back to the Priors once the horses are rested. They can be sent for if and when required.'

'A splendid idea,' said Adrian, walking over in time to hear this, 'as was bringing your own mounts. There's the annual horse fair in Canterbury in a few days' time. I thought some of us might ride over and take a look.'

'Gentlemen only, I trust?' grinned Nicholas.

'And a respite from all things festive,' agreed Adrian dryly.

Inside the house, Caroline welcomed the ladies and then, leaving Mrs Holt to show Madeleine to her rooms, took Adeline to settle Vanessa in the nursery. No sooner was this done and she was back downstairs, than Sebastian and Cassie Audley arrived, bringing Lily Brassington with them.

'I thought we'd arrive first,' said Cassie, hugging Caroline. 'I might have guessed that Rock would beat us to it.'

'Only by a whisker,' laughed Caroline, turning to embrace Lady Brassington. 'I'm so glad you finally accepted our invitation, Lily. What changed your mind?'

'When you told me that you had invited your grandfather and I realised you needed an extra lady to balance the party.'

'You know perfectly well that is *not* why we invited you!'

Lady B smiled. 'I do and I thank you. Has Mr Maitland arrived yet?'

'No. We don't expect him until tomorrow.' She stopped, glancing through the window at yet another carriage. 'That must be Lord and Lady Amberley, thus making the party complete for today. I'll leave Mrs Holt to show you and Cassie upstairs while I help Rosalind with the children. There will be tea in the drawing-room when you are ready.'

An hour later, leaving maids and valets busily unpacking, everyone assembled to exchange greetings over tea and cakes. Drawing his wife to his side, Adrian said, 'Caroline and I would like to welcome you all to Sarre Park – and thank you for making the journey at this time of year. We hope to make your stay enjoyable.'

'No fears on that score,' laughed Nicholas. 'Bertrand says he has plans.'

'God help us, then – given his current mood,' muttered Adrian. And to Caroline, 'Please tell me you didn't give him a free hand?'

'Let's just say that I ... promised him a certain amount of latitude.' And turning to their guests, 'Since everyone has been travelling, I thought we might be informal this evening and dine a little later in case any of the children need their mamas before they will settle.'

'Are Julian and Arabella bringing their three?' asked Cassie, reaching for a lemon tart.

'Of course. This will be the first real Christmas those children have ever had – and Arabella and I are agreed that it should be made as magical as possible for them.' Caroline hesitated and then, with a touch of defiance, added, 'All being well, they will be here tomorrow. As will my grandfather.'

'Mr Maitland is coming?' said Sebastian. 'Excellent! I look forward to renewing his acquaintance.' And grinning at Adrian, 'I'll never forget *your* first meeting with him – in particular, the look on your face when you realised who he was.'

'I daresay,' sighed his lordship. 'And hope Mr Maitland's memory is less acute.'

Caroline smiled up at him. 'It isn't. But in this case, it works in your favour.'

* * *

Later that night and alone for the first time that day with her husband, Adeline said, 'Does Caroline suppose that any of us would dream of turning a cold shoulder upon her grandfather? Surely she knows us better than that?'

Rockliffe laid a hand on the ripening swell of her belly, marvelling as he always did at the prospect of the new life due in some three months' time. He said, 'Maitland is a self-made man who has amassed a fortune through hard work and shrewd investments. If I were Caroline, I would be more concerned about how *he* will take to what he may well see as a collection of idle aristocrats.'

'Seriously?'

'Yes. Adrian tells me that the gentleman is alarmingly astute and forthright.' A smile entered the lazy tones. 'He also apparently plays a killing game of piquet. Personally, I am looking forward to testing that.'

* * *

Hubert Maitland's carriage drew up around noon on the following day when most of the gentlemen were out riding and the ladies were playing with the children in the drawing-room. Lady Vanessa Jane, Lady Deborah Ballantyne and Benedict, Viscount Eastry were building a castle out of coloured bricks under the solemn supervision of Lord Mallory, Deborah's three-year-old brother.

The first sound of wheels had Caroline outside on the steps before Mr Maitland had stepped down from the carriage.

'Well now, lass,' he huffed, when she cast herself on him as his foot touched the gravel. 'I was looking forward to having this fancy new butler of yours bow me in.'

She laughed. 'I couldn't wait. But he'll bow to you anyway. He always does.'

'Good. Then let's get you out of this perishing wind. Don't want you taking a chill and giving it to young nipperkin, do we?' Tucking her arm in his, he said, 'Am I the last to get here?'

'Not quite. We're still waiting for Lord Chalfont's party.'

'Him being the Virtuoso Earl? The fellow with the orphans?'

'The very one. You'll like him.'

'Aye. I reckon I might at that.'

They had reached the hall and, as predicted, Croft gave a stately bow.

'Welcome, Mr Maitland. Thomas will bring in your bags directly. I trust you had a pleasant journey, sir?'

'No better nor worse than I expected – but I thank you for asking.' And to Caroline, as she drew him towards the stairs, 'Where's that husband of yours?'

'Somewhere on the estate – a problem to do with drainage, I believe. He should be back soon. Meanwhile, Betsy will bring you a pot of tea – she won't allow one of the maids the honour of waiting on you – and you can come down to the drawing-room when you're ready.' She smiled and kissed his cheek. 'Your great-grandson is there.'

An hour later, Hubert Maitland had been introduced to seven ladies – only one of whom wasn't titled. Of course, that hadn't been a surprise. Caroline had made sure he was fully informed about his fellow-guests and so making his bow to a duchess hadn't been either a surprise or even mildly disconcerting. There was, however, one extremely pertinent fact that his grand-daughter *hadn't* mentioned and which hit him like a punch in the chest when he realised it.

It happened as he watched Benedict pick up one of the sturdy wooden soldiers he had just been given and inevitably, at only a year old, use it to bang on the floor. Hubert still found the idea that his great-grandson had been a viscount since birth bizarre – as did the fact that he was currently playing with a three-year-old earl and a duke's tiny daughter. But when, unlike Lady Vanessa Jane, Lord Mallory hadn't also grabbed one of the soldiers but merely stared longingly at the remaining ten, Hubert pushed the box towards him saying, 'There you go, lad. Get them out and lined up for battle, why don't you?'

John beamed and nodded but, instead of immediately sitting down to play, took one and placed it gently in the marchioness's hands, saying, 'See, Mama? Soldiers.'

Hubert Maitland watched the lovely brunette trace the contours of the toy with light fingers while seeming to smile into her son's bright gaze. She said, 'So it is. How kind of Benedict's grandpapa. Say thank you, darling – and remember that you are only borrowing them.'

Although he said nothing, a frown gathered behind Hubert's eyes and, seeing it, Lily Brassington slid into the chair next to his, saying softly, 'Yes. The marchioness is blind.'

'Since birth?' he asked brusquely.

'No. A childhood accident – and nothing to be done about it, despite Lord Amberley's numerous efforts.'

'She hides it very well ... but it must be hard on both her and his lordship.' Then, transferring his attention from the marchioness to the mature but still attractive woman beside him he said, 'You'd be the lady who took my little lass to balls and parties before she wed his lordship.'

'Yes.' Lily smiled. 'And you'd be the gentleman who paid for the awful gowns.'

Hubert blinked and peered at her beneath lowering brows. 'Awful?'

'Quite dreadful, actually.'

'All of them?'

'Every last one.'

He considered this in silence for a moment and then gave a snort of laughter. 'Well, how was I to know?'

'You weren't,' she agreed composedly. 'But the dressmaker should have done. Luckily, Lord Sarre was able to see beyond the clothes to the lovely girl wearing them.'

'Lucky for both of them, I'd say.' He hesitated for a moment. 'Do you take on many girls like my Caroline?'

'One or two each season. My late husband and I were never blessed with children ... but there are always young ladies lacking suitable connections, whose families are happy to pay a small fee for chaperonage and the right invitations.'

He nodded. 'Do you enjoy doing it?'

'Usually, yes – though the girls are not always as pleasant as Caroline.' She bent her head towards him and murmured, 'But when they are not, there is always that small fee.'

Hubert didn't need to ask if she needed the money. She was a widow; and even *he* knew that a lady like her didn't take what amounted to paid employment if it could be avoided. So he said meditatively, 'But that's not the only advantage, is it? Young company and a reason to go out and about, as well. I'd call it a smart choice on your part, my lady. Very smart, if you don't mind me saying.'

Lady Brassington didn't mind. More than that … for the first time in more years than she could remember, she actually felt herself blushing.

Fortunately, Lady Vanessa chose that moment to abandon her soldier in favour of hammering tiny fists on Hubert's knee, saying clearly, 'Up.'

He smiled and tapped her nose. 'Up, young lady?'

She nodded emphatically. 'Up. *Up!*'

On the far side of the room and already half out of her chair, Adeline said, 'Vanessa? Come here, darling and don't pester Benedict's grandpapa.'

'Up,' insisted Vanessa. 'Up. Granpa.'

Cassie and Lily laughed. Helping the child scramble into his lap, Hubert said, 'It's been a good while since a pretty lass wanted to sit on my knee. And you're not pestering, are you, little Miss? You just know what you want.'

'Oh, she does that, all right,' muttered Adeline as Vanessa bounced on Mr Maitland's knee, gleefully trying out her new word over and over again.

'So,' said Hubert, gently prodding her tummy. 'So I'm to be Grandpa, am I?'

'Granpa,' agreed Vanessa, patting his face. 'Yes.'

Which was how it came about that when the gentlemen returned from their ride, his Grace of Rockliffe walked in to find his daughter fast asleep on her newly-adopted grandpapa's chest.

* * *

The Chalfont party finally arrived a bare hour before dinner. Arabella was bright-eyed and laughing; Julian, thoroughly creased and rumpled. Ellie and Rob gazed open-mouthed at the boughs of Yuletide greenery, subtly entwined with gold ribbon and looped up at intervals with big red velvet bows. Tom shoved his hands in his pockets and tried to appear suitably blasé.

'It looks … it's like *magic*,' breathed Ellie. 'Are there fairies?'

Arabella hid a smile and Julian turned a laugh into a cough.

'We're not sure,' whispered Caroline. 'They don't show themselves to grown-up people, you see – only to children. And the other children here are much younger than you so they may not have noticed. But if *you* see any fairies, perhaps you'll tell me?'

'Yes. That is ... I will unless they say it's a secret.'

'Ah. Well in *that* case,' said Adrian, 'it goes without saying that you mustn't tell.' He grinned at Julian, 'You look a trifle the worse for wear.'

'Thank you,' muttered Julian.

'He's had Ellie on his knee for the last two hours,' explained Arabella. 'And poor Rob never travels well. So it's a bath, supper and bed for the pair of them – and no arguments.'

'I'll have dinner set back an extra half-hour,' offered Caroline. 'Croft will have the luggage brought up while Mrs Holt shows you to your rooms. And here are Bertrand and Sarah.' She smiled at Ellie. 'You'll remember Sarah from when you stayed at the duke's house. She's here with --'

'Lady Vanessa Jane?' asked Ellie with a beaming smile.

'Yes – and some other children you haven't met yet.' Sarah took the child's hand. 'You'll be the biggest girl in the nursery, Miss Ellie, so I'm depending on you to be my best helper.'

Ellie nodded vigorously and, talking all the time, let Sarah lead her away.

Bertrand, meanwhile, fixed the boys with an expression of intense concentration ... and launched into one of his favourite games. The result was a rapid speech in such hopelessly mangled English as to be almost completely unintelligible. Tom and Rob gaped at him in confusion while, behind their backs, Caroline struggled not to laugh and Adrian sent Julian and Arabella a conspiratorial wink, along with a quick shake of his head.

When Bertrand finally ran out of steam, Rob looked anxiously at his brother and whispered, '*What* did he say?'

'Shut up,' muttered Tom. And with slow, excruciating courtesy, 'I'm very sorry, sir. We did not quite understand. Did you say you would take us to – to the room of night? Did you mean a bedroom, perhaps?'

'The poor fellow's French,' offered Adrian. 'He means well but you'll have to make allowances.' And swiftly switching languages, 'Did you *have* to do that now, you idiot – before they've even got their coats off?'

'Why not?' shrugged Bertrand. Then, 'The older boy has excellent manners.'

'He does – considering he's probably wondering if he's come to the mad-house. And God knows what Lord and Lady Chalfont are thinking. Put it right, will you?'

Bertrand heaved an immense sigh, grinned and said clearly, 'Spoilsport.'

Rob's jaw dropped afresh. Tom blinked and said uncertainly, 'Who is, sir?'

'Lord Sarre. He is afraid that, like himself, you and your brother do not have the sense of humour. Me, I hope he is wrong because I am planning many games … and it will be a big disappointment if you do not enjoy a joke.'

A broad smile crept over Tom's face but before he could speak, Rob burst out laughing.

'A joke? That's brilliant! I don't know how you did it with a straight face.'

'He's had a lot of practice,' said Adrian dryly. And to Julian, 'Bertrand is, in fact, *not* an imbecile. He has suggested that two young gentlemen of nine and twelve --'

'Thirteen,' corrected Tom.

And, 'Almost ten,' chimed in Rob, not to be outdone.

'Ah. Then obviously Bertrand was quite right when he said you were both too old to be lodged in the nursery suite with the infantry.' This time he looked at Arabella, 'They'll be sharing a room near his own and he'll keep an eye on them – if that is all right with you?'

She watched Tom and Rob turning pink with pride and standing as tall as they could. Then, smiling at Bertrand, she said, 'I'm sure they'll enjoy that immensely. Thank you, monsieur.'

'It is my pleasure.' He bowed slightly. And behind his hand to the boys, 'Do you understand the English saying *"Partners in crime"*?'

Rob shook his head. Tom grinned and said, 'No, sir. But I think I can guess.'

'Very good. You can explain it to your brother. But for now, follow me and I will show you to your quarters.'

CHAPTER TWO

On the following morning, the party went in different directions. Arabella, Madeleine and Cassie elected to drive into Sandwich, accompanied on horseback by Adrian, Lord Amberley and Nicholas. Rockliffe and Adeline took advantage of the fine morning to stroll in the park; Sebastian took Tom and Rob out to the stables to give Bertrand time to set up an afternoon treasure hunt in the gallery; and Caroline, on the point of showing Mr Maitland the most recent changes to the restored north wing, found herself briefly detained by Julian.

Bathing her in a melting, forest-green gaze, he said exactly what she had expected.

'Do you have a harpsichord, my lady?'

She laughed up at him. 'Caroline, if you please! And yes, we do – though I doubt it has been played for years and can't vouch for its condition.'

'So long as nobody's tipped a pint of wine into it and the mice haven't set up home, it's probably all right. Have they?'

Caroline stared at him. 'No. What on earth gave you that idea?'

'The one I inherited at Chalfont. It took months to repair the damage.' He smiled, gave a tiny shrug and added, 'Tuning is easy. If you'll tell me where to find the harpsichord, I'll do it this morning.'

She tucked her hand in his arm. 'In that case, come with me.'

* * *

Upstairs in the nursery, the Marchioness of Amberley could hear Ellie busy 'helping' Sarah, in between playing with Vanessa and ordering John around in the manner of older sisters everywhere.

As soon as Rosalind appeared, however, Ellie remembered her manners and produced a careful, if slightly wobbly, curtsy. Then she waited awkwardly, wondering why John's mama didn't say anything or even look at her.

'Ellie curtsied, Mama,' said John.

'Ah. Of course she did.' Rosalind sank into a graceful curtsy of her own and said, 'Good morning, Ellie. Are the young ones keeping you *very* busy?'

'Yes - but I like helping.' She hesitated and, turning to John, whispered, 'Why did you tell your mama I'd curtsied? You didn't need to. She saw me.'

'No she didn't,' said John, matter-of-factly. 'Mama can't see.'

Ellie opened her mouth, then closed it again. The idea of someone not being able to see was beyond her comprehension. She didn't know what to say ... and had a worrying feeling that anything she *did* say might be wrong. So she stood quite still, her insides knotted with anxiety and waited for someone else to speak.

Rosalind stretched out a hand, seeking for a chair that had been there yesterday and thankfully still was. Sinking on to it, she said, 'It's all right, my dear. You didn't know. Lots of people don't at first. Why don't you come and sit by me?'

Ellie crossed the short space very slowly. She mumbled, 'I don't understand. Can't you see *anything*?'

'No.'

'Not ever?'

'Not now.' Rosalind took the child's fingers in hers. 'When I was about as old as your brother Rob, there was an accident and I was hurt. The doctors tried to make me better but they couldn't.'

Ellie looked at John and then at little Deborah, currently trying to wrest her doll back from Vanessa. This kind, pretty lady was their mama ... but she couldn't see them. Worse, she had *never* seen them – not even once. That seemed more than just not right. It seemed horribly wrong. She said uncertainly, 'So John helps you?'

'Yes. He is very good.' She ruffled her son's hair. 'He never leaves his toys where I might trip over them and knows that furniture mustn't be moved so I always know *exactly* where it is. And he tells me things – like he did just now.'

Ellie absorbed this and finally said, 'Can I help, too? I would like to.' She racked her brains for a moment, then added, 'I could tell you *Figgy the Magic Dog*, if you like. I know it nearly off by heart now.'

Swallowing a shaky laugh, Rosalind put her arm about the little girl. 'I'd like that very much, darling. Thank you.'

It was several hours later before Ellie remembered something Mama-Belle had said ... something that might mean she really *could* help. She turned it over and over in her mind until it occurred to her that her idea would stand a better chance if other people joined in. Smiling, she ran off to find her brothers.

* * *

Bertrand's afternoon treasure hunt was to take place in the long gallery – once the province of damp, mildew and mice but now largely restored to its former glory and hung with those of the family portraits which had survived the rot.

Knowing that only four of the children were old enough to play and aware of the varying ages, Bertrand had devised a different trail for each child. Tom's clues were blue, Rob's green, Ellie's pink and John, assisted by Caroline, had yellow ones. Each clue – hidden inside vases, behind curtains or pictures or under the seats of chairs – led to the next or sometimes to a sweetmeat or other small prize.

Having been ordered to remain within call in the drawing-room because some clues required their participation, the adults chatted in a desultory fashion against the sounds of laughter, shouting, running feet and sundry collisions coming from the gallery.

Sebastian asked Julian how his concert at the Queen's House had gone.

'Well enough, I suppose. They seemed to enjoy it.'

'And how was the Queen?'

'She was ... very kind.' Apparently feeling something more was required, Julian scraped his mind and eventually came up with, 'She reminded me of Miss Bea.'

Since Beatrice Caldercott was a middle-aged spinster who persisted in patting Julian's hand and calling him a dear boy, this was a source of some amusement. But Adrian said merely, 'Do you have any future engagements?'

'I'll be playing at the gala opening of Vauxhall in April. And I've had a handful of enquiries from elsewhere for the spring … but nothing is definite yet.'

'What he has *had*,' corrected Arabella firmly, 'are requests from two venues in Paris and a third in Vienna. And they are *quite* definite. The only thing left to be agreed is Julian's fee because impresarios offer the least they think they can get away with and hope that the artists don't quibble. Fortunately for us and *un*fortunately for them, Rockliffe's man-of-law, Mr Osborne, is dealing with them on Julian's behalf.'

'And enjoying it immensely,' began the duke, then stopped as Bertrand appeared in the doorway to inform them that it was their turn to join in the fun.

This was to begin with Julian playing well-known nursery songs while Sebastian, Nicholas or Rockliffe, sang the words but left the last line to be supplied by one or other of the children. After that, Adrian was instructed to re-create his role as the hypochondriac, turning the apothecary's bills into four arithmetical puzzles tailored to the abilities of the contestants. Cassie, Caroline and Madeleine got the hilarious task of leading all the children through the first two figures of the quadrille. And the adults competed with each other to supply the silliest wrong answer to a series of riddles – with the result that, by the time all the children had solved their last clue, the entire party was weak with laughter.

Tom was declared the winner with Rob, Ellie and John coming equal second.

Bertrand received thanks and praise with becoming modesty. Then, combining a bland tone with a suspiciously innocent smile, said, 'I am glad you enjoyed It. I have devised something similar for the adults which we will play on the first wet afternoon. But tomorrow, we shall go to the sea – all but the very youngest children. The older ones will not have seen it before, I think.'

'And not just the children,' said Arabella. '*I* haven't either. Is it far away?'

'Not at all.' It was Adrian who answered her. 'I have a house there – or to be more accurate, Benedict does.'

'This is where Nicholas and I spent the days after our wedding,' announced Madeleine. 'It is in a most beautiful place ... miles and miles of sea and sky. I adored it.'

'As did I,' murmured Nicholas, raising her hand to his lips. And even more softly, 'I have some extremely fond memories of the place.'

Being fairly sure she knew which memories he meant, Madeleine blushed.

Bertrand cleared his throat and said, 'Then our plan is this. The gentlemen may ride if they wish but we will also take carriages. Once at Sandwich Bay, you may walk upon the beach in the bracing sea air --'

'*Bracing* doesn't quite do it justice,' grinned Caroline. 'As Adrian is fond of remarking, this part of Kent is a martyr to the easterly wind. So I advise everyone to wrap up warmly.'

'I was coming to that part,' sniffed Bertrand. 'However ... the children can run and play or hunt for shells on the beach. Those who prefer to enjoy the view in comfort may retire to Devereux House where luncheon will be served in due course. All is arranged.' He swept the assembled company with a glance rather like that of a general inspecting his troops. 'We shall depart promptly at eleven o'clock.'

'Late-comers will be left behind,' added Sebastian helpfully. 'And shot.'

* * *

The following day dawned chilly but dry and the cavalcade finally departed a mere half-hour later than scheduled ... ladies and children crammed into three carriages and all the gentlemen but one riding alongside.

Travelling with Caroline and Mr Maitland, Lily Brassington said, 'I daresay you will have visited Devereux House before, sir.'

'Aye. And Caro's right about the wind. It'll cut you in two if you stand still long enough.'

'True. But it isn't *always* like that,' objected Caroline.

'Well that's how it was the day *I* went there – and that was April, not December. So I'll be looking at the sea through a window and over a nice cup of tea, thank you very much. What's more,' he said to Lily, 'I'll lay odds that two minutes after your ladyship's stepped down from the carriage, you'll be joining me.'

Privately Lily thought that enjoying the view over tea with Mr Maitland was a much more attractive prospect than standing outside, holding on to her hat. But she said merely, 'Thank you, sir. I shall bear that in mind.' And to Caroline, 'I gather from what his lordship said that the property is entailed?'

'Yes. It was Adrian's from birth and is now Ben's, though he's a little young to appreciate it yet. But Adrian has always loved the place and we were extremely happy while we were living there. In some ways, I was sorry we had to leave it ... but of course, as the earl, it was necessary for Adrian to live at Sarre Park.'

Lily nodded and asked carefully, 'Will the dowager countess be joining the party over Christmas?'

Mr Maitland gave a derisive snort.

'No,' replied Caroline coolly. 'Her relationship with Adrian has never been close. And although we call on her from time to time, she chooses not to visit.'

'Best thing all round, if you ask me,' muttered her grandfather. 'Not as I've ever met the lady. But I've heard enough to know that the way she and the late earl treated his young lordship was a damned disgrace – if you'll pardon my language.'

For a moment, neither lady spoke but finally, reading Caroline's expression, Lily said pacifically, 'Well, no one can choose their relations ... which in some cases is a pity. And very few families are perfect.'

* * *

Riders and carriages pulled into the yard of Devereux House some twenty minutes later. While the gentlemen helped Mr Clayton with the stabling of their horses and the ladies admired the charming, irregularly shaped house and peered into the walled garden, Tom, Rob and Ellie hurtled to the gate to stare wordlessly over miles of empty grey sea.

'It looks like it goes on forever,' breathed Rob. 'Does it?'

'Not quite.' With Arabella on his arm, Julian came to stand beside them and pointed to the horizon. 'France is somewhere over there.'

'How far away?' asked Tom.

'From here? Not very far. About twenty-five miles, I think.' He looked down at Arabella. 'I hadn't realised you'd never seen the sea. What do you think of it?'

She drew a long breath of the crisp, salty air and smiled.

'I think it's wonderful. Just as Madeleine said; vast and – and somehow eternal.'

'Eternal? Yes. I suppose it is. Do you want to – *aargh*!' He stopped, lurching forward as something hit him squarely in the back.

Arabella and Rob turned, laughing.

Tom pounced on the ball and kicked it back towards Sebastian, whence it had come. Seeing Nicholas and Adrian approaching across the shingle, Arabella snatched up her skirts and shouted for the children to join her. The ball came back, passing a few feet from her. Diving on it, she snatched it up and took off at a run, hotly pursued by Rob.

'That's cheating,' accused Sebastian, swerving to cut her off. 'Don't just stand there, Tom – get the ball back! This is supposed to be football – not pitch-and-toss.'

Arabella hurled the ball towards Julian. He caught it, dropped it into Ellie's waiting hands and said something only she heard. She nodded and threw with all her might ... in the wrong direction. The ball landed in the sea. Julian groaned.

Ellie looked up with a hopeful smile. 'It's alright, isn't it? You can get it.'

'*I*,' he pointed out, 'wasn't the one who threw it in.'

'No. But you have boots.' She took a couple of steps away from him before turning and saying over her shoulder, 'I think I'll take John to look for shells.'

Aware that Nicholas and Adrian were finding the situation funnier than it actually was, Julian watched the ball bob tauntingly just out of reach.

'Come on, Julian – fetch it before the tide turns,' called Sebastian. 'What's a pair of boots anyway?'

Muttering something rude beneath his breath, Julian waited until the next wave brought the ball back to almost within reach. Then, stepping up to his ankles in salt water, he grabbed it and flung it with hard, deadly accuracy at Sebastian who, being engaged in tossing a joke at Cassie just then, only became aware of it when it hit him in the chest, soaking his cravat.

Fixing Julian with a mock-threatening gaze and tossing the ball from hand to hand, he said silkily, 'I see. Going to play dirty, are we?'

Julian shrugged. 'You wanted the ball. You've got it.'

'Right. If that's the way of it ... name your friends, sir.'

'Tom, Rob and Arabella.'

'Yes!' shouted Tom gleefully. 'We Langhams will *slaughter* 'em!'

'Not a chance.' Sebastian kicked the ball to Adrian, who kicked it to Nicholas ... who missed, thus allowing Arabella to swoop upon it and run. 'Wake up, Nick! And who said mere girls could play anyway?'

'I'm not a *mere* girl,' snapped Arabella, dancing out of Nicholas's way to throw the ball to Tom. 'I have three brothers!'

'And I've got five sisters,' retorted Sebastian. 'Does that make me a lady?'

'No. It just makes you a pain in the - the posterior.'

After which the game became a mad free-for-all.

From the warmth of the parlour, Lily Brassington watched absently as that master of mischief, Sebastian Audley, incited mayhem by deliberately hurling the ball at the Virtuoso Earl. Those not involved in the game were also watching but probably wouldn't stay out in the cold for long ... which meant any chance for private conversation with Mr Maitland was limited. Sipping her tea, she wondered exactly how much that gentleman knew about Lord Sarre. Did he, for example, know that when Caroline had eloped with him she'd thought he was a highwayman called Claude Duvall? Lily suspected not. On the other hand, he clearly *did* know a good deal about what happened directly before Sarre left England. Searching for a roundabout way of asking about this, she said, 'You seem to hold Adrian in some affection.'

'Enough to forgive his fancy vests, yes. When Caroline wrote saying she'd wed an earl, I expected some useless fribble. But the day I first met him he'd been helping repair estate cottages and came in filthy as any farm-hand. More to the point, he's got his head screwed on and he loves my lass. That's as much as I could ask for and more'n I expected. And he deserved better than he ever got from his parents.'

'Oh?' said Lily hopefully.

'Aye.' He fixed her with a very direct stare. 'As you've seen, Caroline won't talk about that – not because she don't know but because his lordship wants it that way – so it's not for me to tell. But I learned about the day that daft girl got herself killed from Bailes, the gardener here. He saw the whole thing and took it to the late earl. Only *he* wasn't listened to any more than young Adrian had been when his parents tossed him out of the country.' Hubert paused, his expression grim. 'Then there was that fellow Sheringham, stirring up the dirt and trying to murder his lordship on his wedding day.'

'He did *what*?'

'Put a bullet in him. You didn't know?'

'No! How on earth did they manage to keep *that* quiet?' She stopped abruptly and sat back in her chair. 'Oh. Of course. They went to Wynstanton Priors after the wedding ... so doubtless Rockliffe took a hand.'

'You could put it that way. It was the duke as dug the bullet out.' He paused, enjoying her stupefied expression. 'Yes. That's what I thought, an' all. But now as I've met the gentleman, I doubt there's much he *can't* do when he puts his mind to it.'

'He has that reputation,' agreed Lily faintly, her gaze once more drifting through the window. 'And here he comes ... with the duchess and marchioness and everyone else not running about like five-year-olds.' She stood up. 'They'll need warming up. I'll ask Mrs Clayton for more tea and something for the children.'

Mr Maitland watched her go. The lady had a trim figure for her age and the unfussy blue woollen gown showed it to advantage. Her face was also pleasing. But what Hubert liked best about her was her unpretentious, down-to-earth attitude; that and the fact that she'd been kind to the grand-daughter of a northern tradesman when he'd wager a good many others hadn't even managed to be polite. She'd said her husband had been dead for eight years. He wondered why she hadn't married again. But then he'd been a widower for nigh on two decades and he hadn't remarried either.

The door opened and his fellow-guests swept in on a tide of laughter and cold air.

'Arabella is mad,' observed Madeleine, laying her cloak aside. 'She will ruin her shoes.'

'So?' shrugged Cassie. 'It looks fun. I'd join in myself if I wasn't increasing.'

'And Sebastian would let you, I suppose?'

'After *his* exploits? He'd be a shocking hypocrite if he didn't. Oh good. Tea. Rosalind ... take this seat by the fire and don't worry about John. Lord Amberley has him.'

The door opened again on Ellie, swiftly followed by Rockliffe and Lord Amberley, carrying his small son.

Ellie tossed her coat and gloves aside and went directly to Rosalind. She said conversationally, 'The sea is very big. And grey like the sky. I think it could be frightening.'

'Yes, I daresay it could,' agreed Rosalind. 'Is that why you are here instead of outside with your brothers?'

'No. I didn't play for long because I threw the ball in the sea by mistake and Sir Julian had to go in the water to get it back.'

'Ah. Was he cross?'

'No. He's never cross. Well, except for the time I tried to take Figgy – that's my *real* dog, not the one in the story – to London after he'd said I couldn't. But even then he wasn't *properly* angry. And he never shouts at any of us – not ever.'

Hearing the wealth of love in the child's voice, Rosalind reached out to take her hand ... and found it wrapped around something. She said, 'Let me guess. Shells from the beach?'

'No. We hardly found any shells but some of the stones are nice. I chose these for you.' She set one in the marchioness's palm. 'Feel how smooth and round it is. And this black one's different. It has lumps and corners. They're dry now. But when they're wet they look shiny and pretty.'

Observing with the marquis from the far side of the room, Rockliffe said lazily, 'It seems that Rosalind has found a new friend.'

Amberley nodded. 'Apparently the child was upset when she learned Rosalind is blind and wants to make it better. Sensibly, she's doing it with small kindnesses.'

'While you're still praying for a miracle?'

'Praying for one, yes. Every day. But I stopped *looking* for one some time ago. It's easier that way – for both of us.'

Bertrand appeared in the doorway to announce that a buffet luncheon was laid out in the dining parlour and added, 'Perhaps someone will communicate this to the crazy ones on the beach? They must have worked up an appetite by now.'

They had. All of them trooped in, flushed, laughing and completely dishevelled.

Arabella sent the boys to wash their hands while she attempted, without much success, to tame her hair. Caroline, Cassie and Madeleine shook their heads over the state of their husbands' coats and cravats. Julian surveyed the white water-marks on his boots and sighed. But then, he thought … what *were* a pair of boots compared to a child's complete faith in oneself?

* * *

The journey back later in the afternoon was accomplished in a state of relaxed bonhomie and relative peace. The gentlemen passed the ride making plans for the following day's expedition to the Canterbury horse fair while the ladies contemplated an hour or so of blissful tranquillity before it was time to dress for dinner. Unfortunately, as soon as she set foot in the hall, Caroline knew that she, at least, wasn't going to get it.

Lying in wait, her back ramrod straight and hands clasped tight at her waist, was Mrs Holt … with Croft three steps behind her looking mildly fraught. Neither boded well.

Caroline watched her guests drift away in the direction of their bedchambers and when there was no one to overhear, said, 'Betsy? What's wrong?'

'Some more guests have arrived.'

'*More*? But everyone is already here.'

24

'The ones you invited are,' came the grim reply. 'These are ones you didn't.'

Caroline stared at her. 'Who, exactly?'

The housekeeper let an ominous pause develop.

'Your ladyship's mother and sisters.'

CHAPTER THREE

'*What*?' gasped Caroline. 'No. They *can't* be!'

'Well, they are. They've brought enough luggage for a fortnight and paid off the coach they came in. I'm sorry to say it, my lady, but I warned you having holly and the like in the house afore Christmas Eve would bring ill luck. And *now* see what comes of it.'

Caroline shut her eyes and groaned.

'Mr Croft let them in – which I'll admit he couldn't avoid,' continued the Voice of Doom, 'But if I hadn't arrived in time, he'd have put them in the best drawing-room. As it is, they're in the old south parlour … not that we can hide them there forever.'

'We can't hide them at *all*. How *can* we? This is a disaster!'

'What is a disaster?' Adrian tossed his gloves on to a table and strolled to her side, smiling. 'Whatever it is, I'm sure we can find a way to mend it.'

'No,' said Caroline, despairingly. 'We can't. Mama and the girls are here.'

The smile evaporated. 'Ah.'

'Exactly.'

'I thought you had explained very clearly that Christmas would not be possible and invited them to join us at Easter instead?'

'I did. But they've come anyway. That would be Mama, of course.' She turned anguished brown eyes on him. 'What on earth are we going to do with them?'

Adrian drew a brief, irritable breath.

'Since we can scarcely send them back to Twickenham, they don't appear to have left us much choice in the matter, do they?'

'Well, we'll have to think of something.' She swung round to the butler. 'Croft. Go and ask if they would like more tea. Do *not* tell them that his lordship and I have returned. And do whatever you must to make sure they stay where they are.'

Croft bowed and tried not to let his relief show.

'Certainly, my lady.'

Mrs Holt sniffed audibly. 'You know the situation with regard to bedchambers, my lady. There's only one fit to use. Shall I send the maids to make the bed up?'

'Not yet. Not unless his lordship and I can find no other alternative.'

'Which I suspect we won't,' murmured Adrian as Betsy curtsied and withdrew. 'I recognise that it's unfortunate but --'

'*Unfortunate*? It's going to be a nightmare! You know what Mama will be like.'

Adrian *did* know and though he said nothing, he had to repress a shudder.

'She'll talk too much and be over-familiar,' continued Caroline. 'She'll wear out everybody's titles but get them wrong most of the time. She'll attach herself to Adeline and Rosalind because of their rank and probably ignore Cassie as being of no consequence. As for grandfather ... I daren't even *think* how she'll behave towards him.' She stopped and spread her hands. 'It will all be embarrassingly awful.'

'Perhaps.' Adrian drew her against him. 'But upsetting yourself isn't going to help. We'll manage the situation somehow. And like it or not, sweetheart, we're going to have to squeeze them in somewhere.'

'Squeeze who in?' asked Bertrand, emerging from the side-door to the stables.

'My mother and sisters,' Caroline said bitterly, reluctantly disengaging herself from her husband. 'All of whom have descended upon us without either invitation or warning.'

'And you don't want them in the house?'

'No. Horrible as it sounds, right now and with the company we already have, I don't.'

'Then it is easy. Tell them there is no room here at Sarre Park ... but they may stay at Devereux House.' He shrugged. 'It does not make the problem go away but ...'

'It drastically reduces it,' finished Adrian, 'in that they won't be here quite *all* of the time. Well done, Bertrand. Send a groom over with their bags and warn Mrs Clayton to expect them later this evening.' He turned back to Caroline. 'They'll have to dine here tonight. Mrs Clayton has had her hands full all day so it's unfair to ask her to do more than prepare bedchambers. We can discuss this more fully later ... but right now, we should go and greet your family before they come looking for us.'

Caroline nodded. 'Thank you, Bertrand. You're a treasure.'

'I know,' he said. 'But butter me up some more, by all means.'

'Don't butter him up,' whispered Adrian as they moved away. 'Just keep him busy. Perhaps that will stop him talking about leaving.'

'*Has* he been talking of it?'

'You didn't know?'

'No. Why would he --? Oh, never mind. I can't think about that now with Mama about to explode out of the south parlour at any minute.'

A quiver of amusement touched Adrian's mouth but he said merely, 'Let me set the tone, will you?'

Caroline slanted a glance of admiring anticipation at him.

'You're going to become the haughty, ice-cold Earl of Sarre?'

'Yes. Unless you have any objection?'

'Goodness no! I love it when you're all lordly and masterful.'

The silver-grey eyes darkened a little. 'Do you? I must remember that.'

In the south parlour, Mrs Hayward presided over the tea tray while her daughters argued over a fashion magazine. When Adrian and Caroline entered, all three froze for a second before simultaneously launching into speech.

'Ladies.' Although Adrian didn't raise his voice, his tone commanded silence. 'This is extremely unexpected. Might I ask why neither Caroline nor I were given any notice of your intention to visit?'

'We took a fancy to surprise you.' Predictably, it was Mrs Hayward – not sounding in the least discomposed – who answered. 'No harm in that, is there? And a mother shouldn't need permission to visit her own daughter, should she?'

'This is not about permission, ma'am. It is about the fact that you were perfectly well aware before you left home that Caroline and I already have a house full of other guests. I am therefore at a loss as to why you might conceivably suppose that this was an appropriate time to ... surprise us. Well?'

Mrs Hayward flushed a little and fiddled with a teaspoon.

'Why wouldn't it be appropriate? What difference can three more make?'

'A great deal,' replied Adrian coolly. 'However, I am still waiting to learn why you are here. It may be only six days to Christmas but I doubt you chose to visit at what you knew to be an inconvenient time purely to wish us the compliments of the season.'

'Inconvenient!' she began. 'What a thing to say to --'

'I'm sorry, Caro,' said Sylvia, cutting her mother short before she could make the situation any worse. 'I tried to talk her out of it but she wouldn't have it – nor Lavvy, either. They got it into their heads that you'd have a lot of single young gentlemen staying and Lavvy and me might find husbands.'

'In that case, it's a pity they didn't write to me,' remarked Caroline calmly. 'I could have saved all of you a wasted journey.'

Lavinia stared at her. 'But it said in the society pages you had a duke and a marquis coming – and that Virtuoso Earl everybody's talking about.'

'All of whom are married.'

'Well, I know that. But you must have *some* gentlemen who aren't.'

'We do. One of them is Adrian's friend, Monsieur Didier.'

Lavinia's expression said, 'That odd French fellow?' even before the words came out of her mouth and were immediately followed by, 'And who's the other one?'

'Grandpapa Maitland.'

There was a brief, catastrophic silence followed by the predictable explosion.

'*Him*?' snapped Mrs Hayward. 'You invited *him* and not your own mother? He's here hobnobbing with dukes and suchlike while your sisters and me was left out in the cold? For shame, our Caro! How *could* you?'

'As a matter of fact, it was I who suggested inviting Mr Maitland,' said Adrian. 'I have a great respect for him and thought this was a good opportunity for us to become better acquainted. But that is beside the point at present. Our difficulty is that we don't have sufficient suitable bedchambers to accommodate three additional guests.'

Mrs Hayward's angry, 'How can that be?' clashed with Lavinia's incredulous, 'You're saying we can't stop here?' both nearly drowning out Sylvia's muttered, 'Told you, Mam.'

Adrian, in the chilly persona of the Earl of Sarre, stared all three of them down.

Then, as he was about to speak, Mrs Hayward put both feet in her mouth. She said, 'No room, my lord? In a house *this* size? I don't believe it.'

The chilly gaze became positively arctic. 'Indeed?'

'Shut up, Mam,' hissed Sylvia. 'You're not helping.'

'I'm only calling it as I see it.'

Adrian let her words hover on the air for a moment.

'Then permit me to do the same, madam. I do not take kindly to being called a liar.'

'And neither do I on his behalf, Mama,' said Caroline crisply. 'We had a solution to this difficulty. But if this is how you mean to conduct yourself, it might be best if you removed to the King's Arms in town.'

Belatedly recognising her mistake, Mrs Hayward said disjointedly, 'I didn't say he'd lied, Caro. My lord, I wouldn't never ... you've mistook my meaning.'

'I would certainly hope so.' He turned to Caroline, allowing her to glimpse the sardonic devilment lurking behind his eyes. 'Well, my love? What shall it be?'

Caroline thought rapidly. It would be Devereux House of course because she couldn't, in all conscience, send them to an inn. But neither could she let them loose on her other guests without making a few things crystal clear.

'We'll come to that in a moment.' She looked unsmilingly at her mother and sisters. 'It goes without saying that you are my family and I love you – but you should have stopped to think before descending on us without warning. Although nothing will be said about it, all our guests will realise what you've done. *They* will be at pains not to cause embarrassment under our roof ... and I'd like to be assured that the same will be true of you.'

'You don't need to tell us that,' objected Lavinia huffily.

'I'm sorry but I do. Take yourself, for example. There are a number of extremely good-looking gentlemen in the house, all of them married. Making sheep's eyes at them --'

'I wouldn't!'

'Yes, Lavinia, you would – and it won't do you any good. The gentlemen will pretend not to notice and their wives will either be irritated or, worse still, amused.' Seeing her sister effectively silenced, Caroline turned her attention to Mrs Hayward. 'All our guests have impeccable manners and will be unfailingly polite. But don't mistake that for a desire to become your bosom friend. It isn't. So please just show a little circumspection and – and try not to talk too much.'

'I'll not be spoken to like that!' Mrs Hayward's colour had risen again and she bristled with indignation. 'I may not be a duchess but there's nothing wrong with *my* manners. And as for talking too much --'

'You do, Mam,' interposed Sylvia, laying a restraining hand on her mother's arm. 'Sorry to say it, but our Caro's right. Folk here'll like you better if you don't go boring 'em to death.'

'Thank you, Sylvia.' Caroline summoned a smile. 'For the rest, though we can't accommodate you here at Sarre Park, there is plenty of room at Devereux House. It is only five miles away, so a carriage can be sent to bring you here from time to time to join the festivities. How does that sound?'

Although looking less than thrilled, Lavinia at least had the sense to know that five miles away was better than going home. Consequently, before her mother could put her foot in it yet again, she said quickly, 'It sounds fine. What do you think, Syl?'

'I agree. Thank you, Caro – and you, my lord.'

'That's settled, then,' said Caroline, trying not to sound relieved. 'You will have the place to yourselves and Mrs Clayton, the housekeeper, will make you very welcome. But to give her time to prepare for your arrival, it will be best if you dine here this evening.'

Lavinia's expression brightened considerably.

Mrs Hayward said grudgingly, 'Well, that's more like it. I suppose you *can* find us somewhere to wash and change – if it's not too much trouble?'

Deciding this was his cue to re-enter the lists, Adrian said pleasantly, 'Mrs Holt will see to it. Unfortunately, however, your trunks are already on their way to Devereux House.' He offered Caroline his arm. 'My dear, there are a great number of matters requiring our attention just now. I'm sure the ladies will forgive us.' And without waiting for a response and with the slightest of bows, he strolled from the room.

As soon as the door closed behind them, he grinned and said, 'Well, that was straight from the shoulder, wasn't it?'

'Yes. But better coming from me than from you, I thought.' She looked up at him, frowning slightly, 'Was it too much?'

'Not at all. It needed saying and I applaud you for grasping the nettle.'

'Thank you. Now all we have to do is hope it has some effect.'

* * *

Caroline took the precaution of warning her grandfather about the new arrivals. Keeping most of what he was thinking to himself, he said, 'That woman never did have more gumption than a flea. But don't worry on my account, lass. In fact, I don't reckon you need to worry at all. When they realise what kind of company they're in, your sisters will be scared of putting a foot wrong. And if your mother behaves like a witless ninny, your friends will pretend not to notice. What they *won't* do is think the worse of you. And they've been welcoming enough with me, haven't they? Never thought *I'd* sit down to a game of cards with a duke.'

Caroline smiled. 'How is that going?'

'One win apiece so far. Now … off you go, lass. It'll be easier than you think.'

As it turned out, Mr Maitland was right. After exchanging nods of acknowledgement, he and Mrs Hayward tacitly ignored each other. None of the other guests revealed the least surprise at the unexpected arrivals. They merely smiled pleasantly, spoke briefly with the newcomers and then carried on precisely as they usually did. Gradually, Caroline felt her nerves unknotting. Dinner passed without awkwardness – if one didn't count Mama spilling a glass of wine over Lord Nicholas's sleeve, an incident he brushed aside with an easy remark, a smile and the use of Mama's napkin along with his own.

Back in the drawing-room with the ladies and under cover of a light-hearted conversation with Mr Audley, Bertrand found his eyes being constantly drawn towards Caroline's sisters. Both of them were pretty; dark hair, deep blue eyes and neat figures. But the younger had something the elder didn't ... and he couldn't decide what it was or why it hadn't struck him on the three previous occasions that their paths had briefly crossed.

According to Adrian, Caroline had read the riot act to her surprise guests and, so far, it looked as if it was working. Mrs Hayward was sitting with Lily Brassington, the only lady present with whom she had some slight acquaintance, but mercifully *not* talking non-stop. The sisters sat side by side on a sofa, apparently rendered mute by Rockliffe's mere presence and the duchess's effortless elegance. He saw Sylvia's face light up when Madeleine took a seat nearby and spoke to them; he watched her ask a question which, judging from the response, was about Madeleine's amber silk gown; and a little later he heard her laughing. It was at that point that he stopped wondering why she was holding his attention and started feeling discomposed by it.

This was compounded when Adrian emerged at his side and asked him to escort the Hayward ladies to Devereux House.

Bertrand scowled. 'Is that really necessary?'

'Caroline thinks so. And I suppose someone should introduce them to Mrs Clayton.'

A long-suffering sigh joined the scowl. Sebastian laughed.

'Where's the problem, Bertrand? You've been ogling the younger Miss Hayward all the time we've been talking.'

'I have not!'

'Yes, you have. And now Adrian's giving you a chance to do it at closer quarters.'

Bertrand swore beneath his breath and stalked off.

'Was he?' asked Adrian interestedly.

'Yes. And not being nearly as subtle about it as he thought.'

With a coachman and groom on the box, Bertrand had no choice but to join the ladies inside the carriage. This, since there were four of them, resulted in him sharing the backward-facing seat with Sylvia … who showed every sign of pretending he wasn't there. Telling himself that this was just fine with him and that the faint perfume of her hair was *not* teasing him to lean closer, Bertrand folded his arms and stared out into the dark.

Freed from her best behaviour, Mrs Hayward had a great deal to say about heartless, ungrateful daughters who denied their mothers a bed beneath their own roofs. Her daughters allowed her to ramble on for a time but finally Sylvia cut across the litany of complaint to say bluntly, 'Stop it, Mam. I told you over and over that we shouldn't come but you wouldn't listen and this is what's come of it. So why don't you look on the bright side for once? We may not be staying at Sarre Park but we're *staying*, aren't we? And you just had dinner sitting next to the brother of a *duke* – though it's a pity you threw wine over him.'

'I never *threw* it--'

'He took it well though, didn't he? Very gentleman-like, I thought.' Lavinia sighed. 'And he's *gorgeous*-looking, isn't he?'

'Gorgeous,' agreed Sylvia aridly. 'Just like the duke, the marquis, the Virtuoso Earl and Mr Audley. As good a collection of handsome men as you'll find anywhere – and every one of them married.'

'More's the pity,' sniffed Mrs Hayward.

'Then maybe we ought to try making friends with the wives … learning better manners from them, too. They all seemed nice. And Lady Madeleine was lovely to Lavvy and me.'

'Lady Nicholas,' corrected Bertrand, sounding bored.

Turning, Sylvia looked directly at him for the first time. 'What?'

'Madeleine is correctly addressed as Lady Nicholas.'

'And you'd know, I suppose?' This from Mrs Hayward.

He shrugged and said nothing.

'Lady Nicholas sounds funny,' said Lavinia doubtfully. 'Are you sure?'

'Yes. Madeleine has no title in her own right. Her husband is *Lord* Nicholas, this being the courtesy title of a duke's brother … and thus making Madeleine *Lady* Nicholas.' He met Sylvia's eyes. 'If you want to learn, begin with the correct forms of address.'

She continued to look at him, unsure whether he was being helpful or provocative. The expression in his eyes – what she could read of it in the shadowy light – suggested the latter. Although she had barely exchanged two words with him in the past, she now had the suddenly disconcerting suspicion that he was a lot cleverer than she'd supposed.

In her usual fashion, Mrs Hayward took the opportunity to return to what she considered the crux of the matter. 'Don't my daughter know *any* single gentlemen, Mr Deeday?'

'Monsieur Didier,' he corrected coolly. 'Di-dee-ay. Perhaps you might try it?'

She gave an outraged splutter. Fortunately, before she could speak, Lavinia giggled and said obediently, 'Monsieur Didier?'

'Yes. Very good, Mademoiselle. You see, Madame? It is not so difficult. However, to answer your question … yes. Caroline and Adrian know a great many unmarried gentlemen. But this party is composed of their closest friends and those friends' children.'

'So that's that, Lavvy. Nobody worth stalking,' remarked Sylvia. And with a sly, slanting smile, 'Unless you want to set your cap at Monsieur Didier here?'

Lavinia's jaw dropped and she struggled to find something to say.

Bertrand had no such difficulty. Turning a blandly mocking gaze on Sylvia, he said softly, 'Since we are being so forthright, I will point out that any pursuit of me would be a waste of *any* lady's time. But I congratulate you on pronouncing my name correctly, Mademoiselle. Well done.' And thought, *So … I am of no account, am I? A joke, in effect. Well, we shall see about that.*

CHAPTER FOUR

On the following morning, most of the gentlemen rode to the horse fair in Canterbury. Only Mr Maitland and Lord Chalfont, neither of whom had any particular interest in horseflesh, remained behind. Mr Maitland sought out Lily Brassington and invited her to drive to Sandwich where they could explore the town and take luncheon. Julian, inevitably, drifted to the harpsichord ... first to give Rob a music lesson and then to delight everyone within earshot with exquisitely played pieces of Bach, Couperin and Scarlatti.

Bertrand leaned against the door-jamb during *Les Barricades Mysterieuses* and, when it finished, strolled in saying, 'Forgive me for disturbing you, my lord.'

His lordship swivelled to face him. 'You're not. I'm not working – merely keeping my hands supple. And it's Julian, if you recall. What can I do for you? Not more nursery tunes, I hope?'

Bertrand inclined his head. 'Julian, then – and no, not that. There is to be ... let us call it an informal soirée ... tomorrow which I shall announce to everyone this evening. I am hoping you will play a few pieces – perhaps including the one I just heard?'

'You don't need to ask. Aside from anything else, I'm in your debt for spending so much time entertaining the boys. They're loving it. And yes, I'll play the Couperin if you like. Anything else?'

'If any of the guests volunteer to sing, may they come to you for accompaniment and perhaps some small amount of rehearsal?'

Julian winced slightly. 'That depends. *Can* any of them sing?'

'I have no idea – which is the fun of it.'

'That's a matter of opinion. But yes. I'll accompany anyone who's half-way decent.' He paused, thinking it over. 'If Rob wants to play, can he?'

'Of course. The more performers, the better. But aside from yourself and Adrian, who will give some of his characters, everyone else is an amateur.'

'I'd gathered that.' And then, 'Characters? What does that mean?'

'You will see.' Bertrand laughed. 'And I can't wait to see his mother-in-law's face.'

Ten minutes after Bertrand left, Arabella arrived to perch on the bench beside him. Julian slid an arm about her waist and kissed her. She kissed him back before reluctantly pulling away to say, 'Stop for a minute. I need to talk to you.'

Julian nuzzled his way down her neck. 'Later.'

Her brain went fuzzy for an instant but she managed to say, 'It's important.'

'Can I do anything about whatever it is right now?'

'Well, no. But –'

'Then it can be important later.'

Holding him off, Arabella said the one thing guaranteed to get his attention.

'It's about Ellie.'

He went still. 'What about her?'

'Has she asked you to make a special Christmas wish?'

'Oh - that.' Relaxing again, Julian grinned. 'Yes. She told me what to wish for and said it was to be a secret. You, too?'

'Yes. And Tom and Rob – which leads me to suppose she's asked us all to make the *same* wish. If I'm right, she's going to be disappointed … and it's my fault.'

'Is it? Why?'

'I told her that Christmas was a special time when, if one wished for a thing *very* hard, the wish might come true,' sighed Arabella. 'Obviously, I thought she'd wish for something we could give her – probably a goat, since the current love of her life is the one in Adrian's stables. But she's not, is she? She's wishing for something that isn't going to happen.'

'It looks that way. But if you didn't *promise* that her wish would come true --'

'I didn't. I only said that it might. But to Ellie, the difference between *might* and *will* is the equivalent of a split hair.' Arabella leaned her head on his shoulder. 'This is her first Christmas ever, Julian. I don't want it spoiled because I put a silly idea in her head.'

'So distract her with a different one,' he suggested. 'Remind her about the fairies in the hall. That should do the trick.'

'You think so?'

'It's worth a try. But stop blaming yourself. You couldn't know she'd get an idea like this one. And meanwhile, I need you to help me decide what to play at Bertrand's soirée. He has asked for *Les Barricades*. What do you think?'

* * *

On the short carriage ride into Sandwich, Mr Maitland and Lady Brassington discussed the previous day's surprise arrivals and discovered themselves in complete agreement.

'Maria Hayward's daft,' grumbled Hubert, 'and the older girl isn't much better. But barging into a party uninvited? They must be completely addled.'

'Yes. It's clear enough what they hoped for, though.'

'Oh aye. Titled husbands like the one Caroline's got.' He thought for a moment. 'Don't suppose *you* could do anything for 'em, could you?'

'No. Or not what their mother wants,' came the truthful reply. 'Mrs Hayward is aiming too high. And I don't move in the circles where she *should* be shopping.'

'Which are what?'

'Respectable, professional men. Lawyers, doctors, bankers … businessmen of any sort. They don't have titles but they quite often have money. And a pretty wife, loosely-related to an earl wouldn't be an unattractive prospect.' She smiled wryly. 'Unfortunately, nothing and no one is going to convince Mrs Hayward of that.'

They strolled arm in arm along the riverside before turning into the medieval heart of the town. Although dry, the day was growing progressively chillier and, with a knowledgeable glance at the sky, Mr Maitland remarked that snow might be on the way.

'In time for Christmas?' asked Lily.

'I wouldn't be surprised.'

She laughed at him. 'You need not sound so gloomy, sir. Snow would make the perfect festive touch – and the children will love it.'

'I daresay. Have you come across Lord Chalfont's youngsters yet? Nice manners they've got, considering they had no proper parenting until the earl came along.'

'They adore him, don't they? It's really quite touching.'

'Got quite a way about him, that young man,' he agreed. And with a chuckle, 'Maybe that accounts for Miss Ellie being such a funny, serious little thing.'

'Perhaps. But I wonder …' Lily stopped, reconsidering. She had promised the child, hadn't she? And if Mr Maitland's last words meant what she thought they might, so had he. Looking up at the large building in front of them, she took the opportunity to change the subject by asking what it was.

'It's the Guildhall … and that part over there is the courtroom.' Glancing around the cobbled courtyard and settling the scarf more securely around his neck, he said, 'The wind's getting up. Shall we find a warm place by the fire?'

'That would be very agreeable. Where do you suggest?'

'The King's Arms at the other end of town'd probably be best.' He pointed across the road. 'The Old New Inn is cosy enough but not what a lady like you is used to.'

'Mr Maitland, ladies like me lead very narrow lives inside the boundaries of what society considers suitable,' she informed him, tucking her hand through his arm. 'At my age, I think I'm entitled to broaden my horizons, don't you? And cosy sounds exactly right.'

His brows rose and he laughed.

'Well then, m'lady – the Old New Inn it is.'

They shared a settle in a corner by the fire. Lily listed some of society's more ridiculous taboos ... Hubert retaliated with anecdotes featuring 'the stubborn old codgers' who had known him for thirty years and thus never got around to showing him the respect due to their employer. Punctuated by laughter, conversation flowed like water between them.

He watched Lily taking her first ever sip of cider and learning the illicit pleasure of dipping bits of crusty bread in her stew. He wondered again why a warm, pretty woman like her hadn't remarried. Then he wondered something else ... before mentally berating himself as a silly old fool.

* * *

After speaking to Julian, Bertrand spent an hour discussing arrangements for the St Stephen's Day ball with Caroline and Mrs Holt ... at the end of which Caroline said, 'I'll have to invite Mama and the girls to the soirée – which means having them to dine as well and thus giving myself a headache trying to sort out the table-settings.'

'There's the curate,' offered Mrs Holt doubtfully.

'Not the curate. He's dreadfully shy and won't be able to get a word out without stammering. Doctor Bramhall might be a better choice.'

'He might be – except he's away visiting his sister.'

'Away?' gasped Caroline. 'And us with three pregnant ladies in the house?'

'Back on Christmas Eve, so I'm told. But that doesn't help with tomorrow evening.'

'What about Tom and Rob?' suggested Bertrand.

Caroline thought about it. 'Won't they be even more nervous than the curate?'

'Not if they're sitting by the people they know best,' he shrugged. 'And they will be staying up for the soirée because Julian says Rob will want to perform.'

'Well, I suppose it's as good a solution as any. I'll speak to Arabella … but someone had better warn the boys.'

'I will do it. I'm taking them outside now to burn off some energy. I will also be promising them a visit to Deal Castle … though not, as I'd originally thought, tomorrow.'

'Why not?' asked Caroline.

'Because *tomorrow* everyone will be scurrying about like mice in preparation for the soirée.' He stood up, grinning evilly. 'You'll see.'

She shook her head at him, laughing a little.

'I *knew* I shouldn't have given you *carte blanche*. However, going back to Mama and the girls … if I write a note would you mind taking it to Devereux House?'

'Not at all. Someone should make sure that Mrs Clayton is not being unduly put-upon, should they not?' he said smoothly, aware that he now had the perfect excuse for doing what he had intended to do anyway. 'Write your note. I shall go after luncheon.'

* * *

The Hayward ladies had spent the morning pleasantly enough. They'd explored the house, admired the walled garden and taken a short stroll along the beach for a breath of sea air and to enjoy the view. By the time they sat down to luncheon, however, boredom – and therefore discontent – was already fermenting in two of the party.

'You'd think our Caro would've left a carriage for us to use,' grumbled Lavinia. 'Without one, we're stuck here, never seeing a soul.'

'It's only been one morning,' said Sylvia. 'Be fair. Caro wasn't expecting us and --'

'Wasn't expecting us and don't want us, neither,' snapped Mrs Hayward. 'I never thought I'd live to see the day when a daughter of mine'd be so ungrateful.'

'Give her a chance, Mam. And there won't be much going on at Sarre Park today anyway, with all the gentlemen off to Canterbury.'

'All the more reason to send a carriage for us this afternoon, then.' Lavinia was sticking to her point. 'She *said* she would. We could've at least gone over for tea.'

'What she said and what she does are two different things,' replied her mother darkly. 'She'll leave us stranded here as long as it suits her – you mark my words.'

'So where was the point in us coming?'

'There wasn't one,' said Sylvia, rising from the table. 'I told you that. It was stupid pushing our way in when we weren't invited and this is what's come of it. But moaning isn't going to change anything ... so if the two of you want to spend all afternoon doing it, I'll leave you to get on with it.'

Having walked out of the dining parlour without any clear idea of where she was going, Sylvia stood irresolutely in the hall for a moment before snatching up her cloak. The wind was chilly ... but it might blow away some of her growing irritation.

She stood by the gate, staring at the sea and wondered why her mother and sister couldn't seem to grasp one simple fact. Caroline's marriage gave them access to a level of society that was way beyond their expectations ... but it didn't mean that they *belonged* there or ever would. They might, however, achieve a tenuous foothold that didn't rely solely on iron-clad courtesy if Mam and Lavinia would look around them and *learn*. It didn't take a genius to see that this wasn't a world anyone could just shove their way into – on top of which these particular people were a tight-knit group of friends and relatives.

Last night, Sylvia had watched and listened, studying how ladies like Arabella Chalfont and Cassandra Audley moved and spoke and behaved, both with each other and with the gentlemen. She'd left Sarre Park determined to profit from what she had seen – gloomily aware that it would probably be an uphill struggle.

A horseman approached along the lane. Even before he was close enough for her to see him clearly, she knew who it was. Her brother-in-law's peculiar French friend. She wondered what he wanted and then thought grimly, *Let's hope he's bringing good news before Mam drives me demented.*

He slackened his pace, drew the horse to a standstill and nodded to her.

'Mademoiselle Sylvie. You were going somewhere, perhaps?'

'I hadn't decided. This seemed far enough for now.'

'Ah.' He turned away, leading his horse to the stable. 'Of course.'

Having nothing better to do, Sylvia followed him. The amused understanding she had glimpsed in his eyes told her that he knew why she was standing outside in the wind. It didn't surprise her. She had realised last night that, though he might be odd, he wasn't at all stupid. He was also, when not standing beside men like Lord Nicholas or Mr Audley, not unattractive. Not eye-catchingly handsome either, of course. But she suspected that slender build was deceptive; and the sandy-coloured hair and hazel eyes were accompanied by surprisingly good bones.

For want of something better, she said, 'Is Sylvie my name in French?'

'Yes.' He tossed a gleaming smile over his shoulder. 'Do you like it?'

That smile caught her unawares. She said, 'Yes. It's pretty.' And, startling herself even more, thought, *At least it's pretty the way you say it.*

'So it is.' Seeing no sign of Clayton, Bertrand set about making his horse comfortable. He wondered what she was waiting for. He didn't think she'd followed him for a chat. On the other hand, she was giving him the chance to make her question her unthinking dismissal of him so he said pleasantly, 'Is there something I may do for you, mademoiselle?'

Numerous thoughts collided in Sylvia's head. Monsieur Didier was acquainted with everyone in the house party and seemed to be on easy terms with all of them. He would know the things she didn't; things that could help her. The question, after her silly, would-be clever remark last night, was whether he would. Right now, for example, the fact that he wasn't unsaddling his horse told her he intended this visit to be a short one.

Deciding honesty would work best, she said bluntly, 'I know we shouldn't be here – and if I'd been listened to, we wouldn't be. But now we *are* here I don't want us making fools of ourselves … and after what you said about Lady Nicholas, I wondered what else we'd get wrong. The duke and duchess, for example. What do we call them?'

Hiding the fact that she had surprised him, he said, 'Your Grace. But only the first time. After that, sir and ma'am will do.'

She nodded. 'Thank you. Any others?'

Bertrand passed the guests under swift mental review. 'The gentleman you know as the Virtuoso Earl does not use his title. He will tell you to call him Julian but it will be more *convenable* if you address him as Mr Langham. And now, if you will forgive me, I must discover if Mrs Clayton has everything she needs to ensure your comfort.'

'Better not let Mam or Lavinia see you, then,' muttered Sylvia darkly. 'If they do, you'll spend the next hour listening to them complaining.'

One brow rose a little. 'So that *is* why you are out here?'

'Yes. But you'd already guessed that.'

'I had.'

'It's only been half a day but they've already started moaning.'

'And it will only get worse?' Since she had fallen into step with him, he felt obliged to offer his arm. *'Bien sûr, mademoiselle*. But perhaps I can mend matters.'

She grimaced. 'Have you got a magic wand in your pocket?'

Bertrand smiled and shook his head. 'Not today.'

'Then you've no chance.'

'Do not be so sure. I shall melt Madame Hayward with my immense charm and --' He paused as she gave a choke of startled laughter. 'You doubt me? You think I can't do it? I am mortally wounded, mademoiselle.'

'No you're not. But it's not just you. The truth is I don't think *anyone* can do it.'

'That is your mistake, then. You forget that I am French.'

No I don't, thought Sylvia involuntarily. *I don't forget it for a second. No one could.*

But she shook her head and said prosaically, 'That wouldn't do you any good with Mam, even on a good day. And right now she's as cross as two sticks.'

'Ah.' Bertrand pulled the note from his pocket. 'Then it is lucky I also have this.'

Her face brightening, she said, 'From Caro?' And when he nodded, 'Thank God! Please, *please* take it to Mam this minute!'

As soon as they entered the parlour, Mrs Hayward surged to her feet saying, 'Well – and about time. Caro and his lordship remembered we're here, have they?'

With a slight, graceful bow and ignoring her question, he said, 'Good afternoon, madame. May I ask if your accommodations are to your satisfaction?'

'They're well enough, I suppose – but they'd be a whole lot better if we wasn't trapped here. Have you brought us a carriage?'

He blinked. 'I am afraid not. But I --'

'Well, is Caro planning to send one, then?'

'She has not spoken of it to me but --'

'So we're just stuck in the back of beyond, are we?' demanded Lavinia sulkily. 'There's nothing for miles around – not even a house, let alone a shop. It's *boring*.'

'Maybe it'd be a good idea to let Monsieur Didier finish a sentence?' suggested Sylvia acidly. 'He's brought a letter from Caro.'

'Oh. Well, why didn't he just say so, then?'

'He might've if you'd given him the chance.'

Seeing them about to start bickering, Bertrand put the note in Mrs Hayward's hand, saying, 'I will leave you to read it while I speak with Mrs Clayton. Excuse me.'

'Wait a bit.' Having broken the seal, she read the brief message and then looked up, her expression one of suspicion. 'Caroline's invited us to dinner tomorrow evening and a … a soyree after it. What's that when it's at home?'

A faint spasm of pain crossed Bertrand's face. He said, 'A *soirée* is an evening party where the entertainment is often provided by guests performing for each other.'

'Performing?' echoed Lavinia. 'Doing what?'

'Whatever they choose, Mademoiselle. Some sing, some recite … some do other things entirely.' He shrugged and added negligently, 'For the most part, it is very relaxed and amateur. But we are fortunate that one of the guests is Julian Langham and --'

'The Virtuoso Earl?' Lavinia was on her feet, hands clasped at her bosom and all trace of sulkiness gone. 'He'll play?'

Bertrand smiled at her. 'He will.'

'Oh Mam! Do you hear that? The Virtuoso Earl! Mrs Walton next door is never going to believe it. Everybody we know'll be green with envy!'

Mrs Hayward's expression thawed and grew thoughtful.

'Yes. I reckon they will at that. What's more, I daresay it'll likely be the earl playing for them as sing. So you and Syl ought to sing summat together. *That*'d get you noticed!'

Sylvia groaned and even Lavinia looked dubious.

Seeing this and simultaneously seizing his chance to get a word in, Bertrand said smoothly, 'Before I leave you to pen your note, Madame … I am arranging a small expedition to Deal the day after tomorrow. If you ladies care to join it, I will have a carriage collect you at eleven o'clock.'

Lavinia's 'Where's Deal?' clashed with her mother's suspicious, '*How* small?'

Since the party might be limited to Tom, Rob and himself, Bertrand chose to answer Lavinia. 'It is on the coast, a short distance from here. Once there, everyone will be free to do whatever they choose. Lord Chalfont's children are eager to see the castle, of course. But there is a pleasant promenade along the seafront and --'

'Shops?' demanded Lavinia.

He inclined his head. 'Certainly there are shops.'

'That settles it, then,' observed Sylvia, only half under her breath. 'If there are shops, wild horses wouldn't keep them at home.'

'Excellent. Then perhaps I may now consult with Mrs Clayton? And no, Madame Hayward – I will *not* forget to collect your note.'

Mrs Clayton having assured him that she had sufficient help and that everything was running smoothly, Bertrand was reluctantly re-tracing his steps to the parlour when he found himself intercepted by Sylvia who said baldly, 'Here's the note for Caro. And thank you for inviting us to join your excursion. You probably didn't have to.'

'No. I didn't *have* to,' he agreed pleasantly. 'But why would I not wish to?'

'Because of what I said last night,' she replied. 'If I offended you – and I think I did – I'm sorry. It was nothing to do with you, really. I was just teasing Lavinia. It wasn't – I certainly didn't mean to insult you.'

'Of course not.' He hadn't expected her to refer to last night at all. He certainly hadn't expected her to take the bull by the horns and apologise. It left him feeling strangely wary – though he had no idea *why* it did. Keeping his smile friendly but not encouraging, he said, 'You make too much of it, mademoiselle. Please put it from your mind.'

Suddenly on the wrong side of an invisible wall, Sylvia was dismayed by how little she liked it. She murmured colourlessly, 'Thank you.'

'Not at all. And now I must take my leave.' He bowed slightly. 'We shall look forward to seeing you all tomorrow evening. *Au revoir, mademoiselle.*'

'Wait!' blurted Sylvia, as he turned away.

'Yes?' Bertrand halted and looked back at her, his expression polite yet cautious.

'Can I visit the castle with the children?'

His brows rose. 'If you wish. But won't you perhaps find it boring?'

'*Boring*? No. I've never even *seen* a castle except for pictures in books – let alone had the chance to actually go *inside* one,' she said. And thought, *Then again, the children won't care if I say the wrong thing in the wrong accent. And maybe … well, maybe I wouldn't mind getting to know you a bit better as well.* Abruptly aware that he was regarding her rather oddly, she added desperately, 'And if you really want to know what I *would* find boring, it's trailing around the shops with Lavinia. She dithers and chatters until I want to scream.'

He laughed, nodded and left. Then he spent the ride back to Sarre Park wondering how much her request to visit Deal Castle had to do with her sister … and whether any small part of it had to do with

44

himself. And then refused to ask himself whether or not he hoped it had.

* * *

Lady B and Mr Maitland arrived back at Sarre Park, arm in arm and laughing, causing Caroline to draw Cassie to one side and whisper, 'Look at Lily. I've never seen her so carefree and – and *young*. Do you think there might be something going on there?'

'I wouldn't be surprised.' Cassie laughed. 'Your grandfather looks as if he's shed ten years as well. A bit of flirtation works wonders, doesn't it?'

The gentlemen returned from Canterbury and sauntered in listening with amusement to Nicholas's attempt to convince his brother that the horse he had bought was worth the price he'd paid for it. Sighing languidly, Rockliffe said, 'Since, personally, I wouldn't have bought the horse at *all*, the price is immaterial, is it not?'

'You were the one who brought the subject up,' retorted Nicholas.

'A mistake, I admit. I ought to have foreseen you becoming tedious about it.'

'Give it up, Nick,' advised Sebastian, laughing. 'It's an argument you'll never win.'

'Oh I know that. Any minute now one of you is going to point out I should know better than argue with Rock about horseflesh.' He impaled the duke with a challenging stare. 'Don't try and pretend *you've* never made a mistake!'

Rockliffe appeared to contemplate the matter and, at length, said, 'Do you know … I don't believe I ever did so. How very trying that must be for you.'

'For all of us,' remarked Adrian over the general laughter.

As everyone settled down to take tea, Julian strolled in with Ellie clinging to one hand. She said, 'I don't think I'm *ever* going to see a fairy. There's always too many grown-ups about. It's a waste of time looking.'

'Then perhaps you and I should come down in the dead of night while everyone is sleeping,' suggested Julian seriously. 'What do you think?'

Ellie shook her head. 'They'd know you were there.'

'Even if I was very, very quiet and kept my eyes closed?'

'I don't know. Maybe. I'll think about it and let you know.'

He grinned at her. 'That's very generous. Thank you.'

She laughed and threw her arms about his waist to hug him.

Last to join the party was Bertrand who, having accepted a cup of tea and made short work of a slice of fruit cake, said, 'May I have everyone's attention?' And when they had fallen silent, 'Tonight will merely be cards and parlour games.' He paused to allow the collective groan to pass. 'I am told that Lady Amberley reigns supreme at Blind Man's Buff ... so we will have a round of that to begin.'

'Excellent!' exclaimed Rosalind. 'None of you stand a chance!'

'Can I play?' asked Ellie eagerly. 'And Tom and Rob?'

'Of course,' agreed Bertrand. 'The more, the merrier. Now ... tomorrow evening we will be holding an informal soirée. I shall expect each of you to volunteer.'

'*All* of us?' asked Nicholas. 'Seriously?'

'Seriously. Everyone will do *something*, however small. Working in pairs is allowed and singers may apply to Julian for accompaniment if they require it ... but everything else must be kept secret.' He grinned around him. 'You have all day tomorrow in which to prepare. *Bon chance, mes enfants*!'

CHAPTER FIVE

With a mixture of amusement and trepidation, Caroline saw that Bertrand had not exaggerated. After breakfast, Nicholas and Madeleine, Lady B and Grandpa Maitland all vanished to their respective rooms; Rockliffe took possession of the library; and everyone else either gathered in corners whispering to each other or descended on Julian.

During the course of an hour's aural torture, his lordship gently but firmly sent all but three of the would-be singers away to come up with an alternative. Two of those were Cassie and Arabella – neither of them remotely surprised or even offended by Julian's verdict, although Arabella threatened him with dire reprisals later. They then spent an hour proposing and discarding alternative ideas until inspiration finally struck and sent them in search of Caroline.

A short time later, the sound of something resembling the cackling of hens caused Adrian to hesitate, wincing, outside the door to his and his wife's rooms. He didn't know what Caroline was up to and backed away, not sure that he wanted to.

After a preliminary rehearsal with the singers, Julian decreed that the next hour belonged to Rob and was just about to sit down with the boy when Mr Audley poked his head around the door, saying, 'Sorry, Rob. I promise I'll be quick. Julian … aside from Rob, the only one brave – or idiotic enough to go anywhere near a harpsichord while you're within earshot is me. And everyone knows I never mind making an ass of myself.'

'You're volunteering to play?'

'In a manner of speaking. But I wondered if we mightn't … elaborate on it a bit.'

The dark green eyes grew suspicious. 'How, exactly?'

'If I play one of the only three tunes I know – it's a reel, by the way – I thought you could add a bit of embellishment. A sort of impromptu duet.'

'Impromptu?' queried Julian. 'Literally?'

Sebastian's assent was drowned by Rob's, 'That'd be brilliant fun! I wish *I* was good enough for a duet.'

'One day,' promised Julian absently. And with a shrug, 'All right, Sebastian. An impromptu duet. You wouldn't also like me to do it blindfold?'

'Blindfold? Now there's an idea. Could you?'

At which point, the Virtuoso Earl told Mr Audley to Go Away, though in words that forced him to add, 'Rob, you didn't --'

'--hear that,' grinned Rob. 'Yes. I know.'

* * *

Conversation over luncheon was all about the things people were *not* doing rather than those they were and most seemed eager to get back to doing them. Cassie, Arabella and Caroline were barely able to stop giggling ... whereas Nicholas and Madeleine had clearly ended the morning on a note of disagreement. Rockliffe, Amberley and Adrian all announced that, being as prepared as they needed to be, they were going riding – which didn't make Nicholas look any happier. And Bertrand asked to be told what the various acts were to be so that he could devise a suitable running order.

Arabella divided the afternoon between rehearsing her own part – which, thanks to Cassie, now involved more than merely learning words – and helping Ellie perfect hers. Julian was kept busy with Rob, the singers and making a final decision on which pieces he himself intended to play. Neither of them knew where Tom was or what he might be planning to do.

In fact, an hour before tea Tom ran Bertrand to earth in Adrian's study and, clutching two sheets of paper in something approaching a death grip, said, 'I want you to read this. I know you said we were just to give you a general idea. But I couldn't think of a single thing I could do that would be any good and wishing I needn't have anything to do with it ... until I realised I was lucky to be here at *all*.' He shoved the paper at Bertrand. 'And – and so I wrote this. It's probably rubbish. If it is, you have to tell me.'

Smoothing the sheets out and absorbing the tension in every line of the boy's body, Bertrand said slowly, 'Tonight is just for fun, Tom. You don't have to do anything you don't want to. If you would rather not perform, you can help me organise things instead.'

'I'd like to do that anyway. But I still want you to read that. Please?'

'Of course.' Waving him towards a chair, Bertrand took the crumpled pages of awkward handwriting and numerous crossings-out to the window and began to read. Five lines were enough to make him glad the boy couldn't see his face; and when he got to the end of it, he

48

had to clear his throat before he dared speak. He said, 'Tom ... do you think you *can* read this out loud?'

'Does that mean I shouldn't? Look – if it's bad, just say so.'

'It is not bad.' Bertrand turned, hoping he had his expression under control. 'It is ... powerful. And if you want to read it, you should. But first let us make sure that you can.' Handing the papers back, he added, 'Read it to me now.'

* * *

At Devereux House, Mrs Hayward and Lavinia debated what to wear that evening at such length that Sylvia's ears began to ache. It wasn't, she reflected, that there was really any decision to be made because they would both wear the most extravagantly modish gowns they had with them; Mam – no – *Mama*, she reminded herself. Mama would be unmissable in her purple silk and Lavinia, beautiful in the cream-and-amber striped polonaise. She, by contrast, had settled on her rose and delphinium watered taffeta which, though it wasn't the newest or most expensive gown she owned, was her favourite and the one which suited her best.

By the time the carriage arrived from Sarre Park, her nerves were at full stretch. Sylvia told herself that this was solely due to the worrying fever pitch of excitement emanating from her mother and sister. Deep down, she knew there was more to it ... but didn't understand *why* there was since Bertrand Didier's opinion of her didn't matter in the slightest. Did it?

Mrs Hayward spent most of the journey badgering both girls to volunteer to sing.

'You've got pretty voices,' she argued, '*and* you know some songs.'

'Country songs, Mam,' said Lavinia dubiously. 'I don't know as they'd suit.'

'Why not? Nobody said it had to be opera, did they?'

Lavinia shook her head. 'What do you think, Syl?'

'I've no more idea than you – so I'd as soon not take the risk.'

'And miss the chance of singing with the Virtuoso Earl?' demanded Mrs Hayward. 'You must have windmills in your head, Syl.'

'Probably. But the evening will go better if we don't put ourselves forward too much,' replied Sylvia flatly. 'And can you *please* call Lavinia and Caroline and me by our full names? You don't hear anybody calling the duchess Addy or the marchioness Roz, do you? And Lavvy and Syl sound horrible.'

'You never minded before,' retorted her mother. 'And don't change the subject. Are you going to sing or not?'

'No,' sighed Sylvia. 'I'm not. But Lavinia can decide for herself.'

* * *

They arrived at Sarre Park to find the rest of the company more than usually animated and already assembled in the drawing-room. While Adrian welcomed them with glasses of sherry, Mrs Hayward exchanged the usual cool nods with Mr Maitland and Sylvia hauled Caroline to one side saying, 'Mama wants Lavinia and me to sing but I've said no. Was I wrong?'

'No.' Caroline laughed a little. 'You've had no chance to practise so no one will be surprised if you don't take part – and in any case, Julian turned down half of those who wanted to sing because he didn't consider them good enough. And now, will you excuse me for a minute while I have a word with his boys? They'll be joining us for dinner to even up the numbers and are probably feeling twitchy about it.'

Caroline soothed Tom's and Rob's anxieties by telling them that one would be seated beside Arabella and the other by Cassie Audley, with Julian and Bertrand close by. 'So you are not to worry. I know you'll behave beautifully and your joining us tonight is a big help.'

Mrs Hayward had been placed between Adrian and Mr Audley so that, as Adrian had said, if she wanted to throw fish in anyone's lap it might as well be either his or Sebastian's. Lavinia was delighted at being escorted in to dinner by Lord Nicholas; and Sylvia felt herself colouring when Bertrand offered his arm, saying, 'Mademoiselle Sylvie ... Caroline tells me that I am to have the honour. Shall we?'

'I ... yes. Thank you.'

Bertrand noticed the blush and wondered what had caused it. Deciding to test the water, he said, 'It is my pleasure. And may I say how very charming you look this evening?'

Catching the faint note of amusement in his voice and feeling her colour rise still further, Sylvia cast him a suspicious glance. 'You can say it if you mean it.'

'What would be the point of saying it if I did not?'

'To tease me? And gentlemen say things they don't mean all the time.'

'Some of the time, I grant you,' he allowed easily. Then, curiously, 'Did Madame your mother succeed in persuading you to sing this evening?'

'No. I've never been to a – a soirée before so I'll be quite happy watching and listening to everybody else. Will you be performing?'

'Perish the thought! I am merely the man who ... pulls the strings, let us say.'

'Like in a puppet show?'

He laughed. 'Yes, mademoiselle. *Just* like that.'

* * *

Dinner passed without any untoward incident and in a mood of steadily growing anticipation. At the end of it, Bertrand rose and, gathering everyone's attention, said, 'This evening, instead of the ladies leaving the gentlemen to their port, you all have a half hour for any last minute preparations. Everyone has a list of which act follows which and if any of you require assistance, speak to Tom or me. And now, unless there are questions, we will re-assemble in the large drawing-room in half an hour.'

With the exception of Rockliffe, Amberley, Adrian, Sebastian and the Hayward ladies, everyone bustled away in various directions. Rising, Adrian smiled at his relations-by-marriage and said, 'There's no reason why *you* should not have tea while you wait. If you care to make your way to the drawing-room I'll have Croft bring some.' And to the gentlemen as the ladies quit the room, 'Equally, if like me, you are left with nothing to do, there is port if you want it.'

'Later,' said Sebastian ruefully. 'If my wits get fuddled, Julian will probably kill me.'

'Only,' murmured Rockliffe, 'if Bertrand does not get to you first. One would think we were all about to grace the stage of the Theatre Royal.'

'He is certainly being very thorough,' agreed Amberley. 'And his insistence on secrecy has added a more than usual note of ... piquancy.'

'You think so?' Adrian glanced from the sheet of paper Bertrand had given him to the duke. 'I could make a fair guess at some of these – as I imagine could you.'

'Oh yes,' agreed Rockliffe. 'But who am I to spoil anyone's fun? And I am *so* looking forward to seeing whatever Nicholas has been coerced into doing. I don't believe he's ever so much as *attended* a soirée – much less performed at one.'

In the drawing-room, Julian strolled towards the harpsichord only to be stopped in his tracks by the look on Rob's face. Pulling the boy down beside him on the bench, he said, 'What's wrong?'

'I can't do it. I – I think I'm going to be sick.'

'Ah.' Julian dropped a casual arm around him. 'Three things, Rob. First, you aren't going to be sick. Second, you don't have to do it if you don't want to. And third --'

'I'm scared I'll get it all wrong!'

'And third, no matter what you decide and even if you don't play it as perfectly as I know you can, I'll still be proud of you.'

Rob heaved an enormous sigh and leaned his head against Julian's shoulder.

'Maybe … if you sit by me like you do in lessons … it might be all right.'

'Then that's what we'll do. In fact, why don't you stay here with me and tell me when it's my turn to do something? I can't remember where I left Bertrand's list.'

The boy sat up, some colour returning to his cheeks. He said, 'It's a good job I've got mine then, isn't it?'

The other guests began wandering back, most taking their seats but others stopping to speak with either Bertrand or Julian. Finally, when everyone except Adeline and Rosalind were present, Bertrand stepped forward and called for silence.

'And now to the moment we have all been waiting for,' he announced with a grin. 'A special treat to begin our entertainment … Louisa and Clara's duet from *The Duenna*.'

And hand in hand from the adjoining room, Adeline and Rosalind emerged to curtsy regally to their audience, to each other … and finally, to Julian, who responded with the opening bars of their introduction.

Both ladies were possessed of clear, true soprano voices which Julian's accompaniment supported rather than overwhelmed. When the duet drew to a close, the applause was genuinely appreciative and Mr Audley began a standing ovation.

Sylvia looked at her mother and muttered, '*That's* why Lavinia and me aren't singing.'

While the duchess and marchioness took their seats and without waiting for Bertrand to announce her, Ellie skipped over to put a sheet of paper in Julian's hand. 'It's me now. Mama-Belle says you're to help if I get stuck – but I won't.'

There was a scattering of laughter over which Bertrand said, 'And now, ladies and gentlemen, a dramatic recitation by Miss Ellie Langham.'

Ellie swished out her pink taffeta skirts, curtsied and began with relish.

'*You spotted snakes with double tongues … thorny hedgehogs be not seen …*'

She recited the poem without hesitation or mistakes and then, before anyone realised she had finished, turned to Julian saying, 'I remembered it all, didn't I?'

He nodded. 'It was so good it was *scary*.'

On her way from the room in the wake of Caroline and Cassie, Arabella paused to give the child a quick hug. 'Well done, darling – listen to them clapping! But you must curtsy and smile, then go back to your seat.'

While everyone was good-naturedly congratulating Ellie, Tom set a small round table centre-stage, put a large cooking pot on it and withdrew.

'Ladies and gentlemen … pray imagine yourselves alone on a cold and windy heath at the dark of the moon,' invited Bertrand chillingly. 'A place of sinister magic and evil spells wrought by ancient crones. Prepare to be chilled by Witches Three. '

'Ooh! Ellie shuddered happily.

'I thought Bertrand wasn't performing tonight,' remarked Sebastian.

Winking at Rob, Julian startled everyone by plunging into the thunderous chord sequence from *Le Vertigo* … while three stooped, black-clad figures glided forth to group around the cauldron.

'*Thrice the brindled cat hath mewed*,' declaimed Cassie, ominously.

'*Thrice and once the hedge-pig whined*,' agreed Caroline with baleful satisfaction.

'*Harper cries, 'Tis time! 'Tis time!*' shrieked Arabella, making everybody jump again.

'I hope nobody's got a weak heart,' muttered Nicholas.

'*Round about the cauldron go*,' chanted all three, suiting action to words. '*In the poisoned entrails throw …*' And on they prowled, tossing dead leaves and bats made of paper into the pot until the final, '*Double, double toil and trouble; Fire burn and cauldron bubble!*' Whereupon they exploded into noisy, raucous cackling – and ran off.

For a couple of seconds there was silence. Then laughter and applause rang out … and, pushing back the hoods of their husbands' cloaks, the ancient crones returned to take their bows.

'Good enough for the Comédie Française?' Caroline asked Adrian presently.

'Not quite,' he replied. And with a grin, 'But you scared the hell out of me.'

While Tom removed the cauldron, Julian looked thoughtfully at Rob and said, 'It's your turn next. What do you want to do?'

Rob hauled in a bracing breath. 'If Ellie can do it, *I* can.'

'Good lad. I'll be right beside you.' He swivelled round, asked Bertrand's permission and then rose to address the audience. 'Ladies and gentlemen, Rob has only been learning to play the harpsichord for a short time and you are privileged to witness his debut performance of a specially arranged piece by Herr Mozart.'

There was a scattering of encouraging applause. Rob took another deep breath, placed his hands on the keyboard … and began. The opening bars were slightly shaky with nerves but the subsequent ones became gradually more confident and during the latter half of the piece, Rob was playing as well as he ever had during lessons. He finished with a whoosh of relief and, turning shining eyes on Julian, said, 'I did it. I really *did* it.'

'You did.' Julian gave him an affectionate nudge. 'Of *course* you did. And listen …'

Sebastian was on his feet, cheering; Bertrand was contributing a few whistles and everyone else was clapping madly. Finding himself pushed off the bench, Rob stood up and, grinning from ear to ear, managed something akin to a bow.

As the room gradually quietened, Rockliffe rose lazily and drawled, 'Well done, Rob … though how I am to follow your performance with my poor efforts, I cannot imagine.'

'Don't overdo it, Rock,' called Nicholas. 'We all know you're an old hand at this. So what's it to be this evening?'

'I shall be delivering a eulogy.' Strolling to centre-stage, the duke waved Bertrand away. 'A solemn and heartfelt *homage* entitled *Upon the Demise of Sartorial Restraint.*' He paused to allow for a few snorts of laughter and added with a faint smile. 'I leave you to determine wherein lies my inspiration.'

'I don't understand,' complained Mrs Hayward, less quietly than she thought. 'What's he talking about?'

'Hush!' hissed Sylvia. 'Hush and listen.'

Giving no sign of having heard, Rockliffe leaned negligently against the mantelpiece and toyed idly with an enamelled snuffbox. Then, in accents of pained resignation, he embarked on a brief and cripplingly funny critique of the Macaroni Club with specific, if unnamed, reference to Viscount Ansford and Charles Fox. By the end of it, half his audience was crying with laughter. His Grace didn't wait for them to applaud. He merely made an extravagant bow and returned to his seat.

The next handful of acts flew by.

The brief scene Nicholas and Madeleine enacted from *The Taming of the Shrew* drew forth numerous teasing remarks about the length of time it had taken Nicholas to persuade Madeleine to accept his suit. Lily Brassington entertained them with Lady Teazle's epilogue from *The*

School for Scandal; Mr Maitland surprised everyone by performing conjuring tricks as *The Great Uberto*; and Lord Amberley delivered the St Crispin's Day speech from Henry V – which, he admitted with an apologetic shrug, had been stuck in his head since Eton.

Accompanied by Julian, Sebastian rollicked his way through *Cuckold's All Awry*, flirting with every lady in turn during each of its many verses. At the end of it and not waiting for the laughter and applause to die away, he waved Julian from the bench and took his place.

'There's a brave fellow,' observed Hubert.

'He is indeed,' agreed Lily. 'Did *you* know about this, Cassie?'

But Cassie merely laughed and shook her head while, without further ado, Sebastian embarked on a fast and furious reel. Julian looked on over folded arms; Ellie bounced on her chair in time to the music; and Bertrand frightened Sylvia silly by pulling her to her feet and twirling her mercilessly round the room.

At the end of it, Julian asked Lily for Lady Teazle's scarf, gestured for Sebastian to make room on the bench and sat down beside him. Then he tied the scarf over his eyes and said calmly, 'Encore?'

The room fell silent and several jaws dropped.

Sebastian stared at him. 'I was joking, you know.'

'Yes. But I'm not.'

'Show-off,' grumbled Sebastian good-humouredly. 'Stealing my thunder?'

Julian shrugged. 'Same speed and you take the first eight bars. *Now.*'

Since he never used sheet music to perform and rarely looked at his hands, playing blindfold was easy ... and made easier by the fact that, since Sebastian only used the lower manual, Julian was able to take sole possession of the upper one. The result, though it amazed the audience, was to him no more than a deceptive trick.

This time, so that Mademoiselle Sylvie didn't get the wrong idea – or even possibly the right one – Bertrand took Ellie for a frenzied gallop before spinning her until she was dizzy. The music ended, Julian and Sebastian shook hands before taking a bow and Rob jumped up and down, cheering.

Aware of what was coming next, Bertrand created a pause by summoning a footman with wine. And when everyone had been served and the excitement had died down to acceptable levels, he announced without any of his previous theatricality that Master Tom Langham had a story to tell them.

'It's not a fairy-tale,' began Tom, matter-of-factly, 'but I'll start it like those stories do anyway. Once upon a time, there were three children – two boys and a girl – and they lived with an old witch in her cottage because their mothers had gone away and their father didn't want them. The witch didn't want them either but she kept them until their father died and she wasn't being paid any more. Then she threw them out.'

Arabella's nerves clenched and she thought, *Oh Tom. You dear, wicked boy.* Peering around Lily Brassington's feathered head-dress, she watched Julian's expression growing increasingly grim as Tom briefly and laconically described how the children had survived months of cold and hunger; how they'd slept in an empty barn and, more often than not, had to steal food if they were not to starve.

'They didn't like thieving but they got pretty good at it. *Had* to when folk started to get wise to them. Then one day a stranger came to live in the house that had been their father's. They didn't know what that meant. They just reckoned it'd be best to stay out of his way. But somebody must've told him about them because, after a bit, he came looking.'

'Over three weeks, Tom,' interposed Julian tightly. 'It took him nearly a month.'

Tom flashed him a small, crooked smile but continued as if he hadn't spoken.

'He said they could live in his house – but that might've been a trick to catch them so they could be split up and sent away and they couldn't let that happen because they'd only got each other. But he didn't come after them. He just put food where they could take it until the two younger ones said a roof and beds were worth the risk.' Tom shrugged and shook his head. 'The oldest boy gave way but he still didn't trust the man. What if he got tired of them? What if he didn't stay? So he kept out of the man's way as much as he could ... until one day the man did something nobody had ever done before. He stood up for the boy when he didn't have to. And he said being a guardian meant protecting all three of them like a proper father would ... and staying with them, no matter what.'

Another fleeting glance in Julian's direction and a brief pause.

'The boy knew the man hadn't got any money. But it took him a long while to understand that the man had given up everything that really mattered to him just by *being* there.' Tom hunched one shoulder. 'He used to say he didn't know anything about children – and maybe he didn't. But he was always patient and he listened and when the children asked questions, he told them the truth.'

Tom folded his papers and shoved them in his pocket, apparently oblivious to the fact that the gentlemen sitting in front of him were tight-jawed, many of the ladies clutched damp handkerchiefs and, behind him, Julian was already on his feet ready to hug him.

'He *still* is all those things. Every day. He's the best example – the best *father* – anyone could have. And that's the end really, except for one thing. I told this story because I couldn't think of anything else to do tonight and because my sister asked me to help her wish for a Christmas miracle. Only I can't do that because I reckon a person only ever gets one of those ... and I've already had mine.'

CHAPTER SIX

Although Lord Sarre's various 'characters' provoked much laughter and, for those previously unaware of his acting ability, great measures of surprise ... and even though Julian's recital could not be other than the crown of the evening, it was Tom's Story that was the topic of most conversations afterwards. And these, inevitably, led Arabella to a worrying discovery which began when Cassie said, 'That was brave of Tom. And the most amazing thing about it was that he wasn't trying to shock or even looking for sympathy – though he got both. It was all about Julian and how much Tom loves him.'

'I know. But what he said at the end about miracles ... how on earth does one reply to something like that? And then there's Ellie. She's furious with him.'

Unexpectedly, Cassie laughed. 'I daresay she is. But she'll get over it. Tell her Tom is only one person and plenty of others have promised to help.'

Arabella stared at her. 'You *know* about that?'

'The Christmas wish? Of course. I imagine everyone does by now.'

'She's asked *everyone*? For the same thing?'

'Yes. At least, she did with Sebastian and me. So I don't suppose she asked Nicholas, Madeleine, Caroline or Adrian for anything different.'

'Oh God,' groaned Arabella.

'She didn't annoy anyone, Belle,' said Cassie quickly. 'We all thought it was rather sweet of her to --'

'That isn't the point. You told her you'd do it, didn't you?'

'Well, yes. She's just a little girl and --'

'Which *is* the point. She's six. She thinks there are fairies in the hall, for heaven's sake. So with everyone in the house promising to help her wish, what do you suppose she believes is going to come of it?'

Cassie opened her mouth, closed it again and finally said, 'Oh.'

'Oh,' agreed Arabella bitterly. 'Forgive me, please. I need to find Julian.'

Having heard her out, Julian said mildly, 'I agree it's unfortunate that Ellie didn't keep it inside the family but --'

'I don't care about that.'

'I know. But aside from talking to her and trying to explain, there isn't much else we can do, is there?' He put his arm around her and dropped a kiss on her hair. 'Worrying won't help, sweetheart. And perhaps visiting the castle tomorrow will take her mind off it.'

* * *

Glad of a quiet day, Lord and Lady Sarre waved their guests off to Deal on the following morning, along with an empty carriage in which to collect the Hayward ladies. Noticing that – in what seemed to have become a habit – her grandfather and Lily Brassington were travelling together, Caroline said, 'This is the third time those two have managed to get a carriage to themselves.'

Adrian grinned. 'Do you think they need a chaperone?'

'Don't be idiotic. But I *am* wondering if anything will come of it.'

'If by that you mean wedding bells, I'd have to say I think it unlikely.'

'Yes,' she agreed reluctantly. 'I suppose so. But you can't deny that they seem to be getting on extraordinarily well.'

'Not well enough to persuade them both to turn their lives upside down.' He caught her fingers in his and pulled her into the house. 'Now … forget them. Do you realise that we have almost an entire day to ourselves?'

'*You* have. *I* have the tenants' baskets to finish before tomorrow. We've packed the meats, pies and puddings that *every* household gets but not the individual items such as scarves or gloves for the elderly and sweets and little toys for the children. So there's still a great deal to do.'

Somewhat uneasily, Adrian wondered how big the baskets actually were. But he said merely, 'Has Betsy got a list?'

'Well, yes. But --'

'Then she can manage without you.'

'Not necessarily,' muttered Caroline.

'What do you mean?'

'She still hasn't got over my bringing greenery into the hall earlier than tradition dictates. *Now* she sees me flouting custom again by delivering the baskets the day before Christmas instead of the day after. She hasn't got to the *Woe Betide!* phase yet but --'

Adrian gave a startled laugh. 'The *what*?'

'No good will come of it, my lady – you mark my words,' recited Caroline in a fair imitation of Betsy's voice. 'I warned you having holly in the house too soon was bad luck. And what happened? Your mother and sisters arrived on the doorstep, that's what!'

'Did she *really* say that?' he asked unsteadily.

'Yes. And it isn't funny.'

Silver-grey eyes alight with hilarity, he said, 'Isn't it?'

Caroline had never been able to resist his laughter. Smiling ruefully back at him, she said, 'Well, all right. Perhaps it is. A bit. But goodness only knows what calamity she'll predict this time.'

'Because,' choked Adrian, 'of the *baskets*?'

'Yes. Never mind that we're holding an informal ball on St Stephen's day and will therefore be somewhat busy. Never *mind* that distributing the baskets on Christmas Eve means everyone will have a better Christmas feast than they would otherwise have done. All Betsy does is shake her head and mutter under her breath. Consequently, if our Yuletide gifts to the tenants are to be ready by tomorrow, I'll need to deal with them myself.'

'Point taken ... but it will wait until later, won't it? Right now, I want you to myself for a little while,' he said, sweeping her towards the stairs, 'and then perhaps a quiet hour with our son. What do you think?'

'I think that, since Ben's favourite thing in the entire world just at the moment is John's toy drum, quiet is the *last* thing it's likely to be,' laughed Caroline. 'But yes. Let's do that.'

* * *

Inside one of the carriages heading for Deal, Lily Brassington turned a mystified gaze on Mr Maitland and said, 'How did you learn to make cards jump out of the pack and things appear seemingly from nowhere? I was never so surprised.'

'Too frivolous for an old self-made tradesman like me, was it?' And as she opened her mouth to deny it, 'It's all right, Lily. I know what I am. As for card tricks and the rest of it, I learned 'em from an uncle who worked in a travelling show. Years later, it came in useful when I started holding Christmas and midsummer parties for the workers and their children.' He leaned back, giving her a thoughtful look. 'But let's not pretend I was the star of the show last night. Aside from young Tom and the Virtuoso Earl, I can't help wondering about Adrian ... and why he winked at you just before he acted the part of that French highwayman fellow.'

'Did he?' Lily did her best to sound baffled. 'I didn't notice.'

'Really? Well, now I'm even *more* curious – not as I haven't always suspected that my grandson-in-law's got a few skeletons he'd like to stay in the closet.'

'I imagine you could say that of most people.'

'Including you?'

'Oh no. Not me.' An arid note entered her voice. 'I have led a thoroughly blameless life with neither misstep nor misadventure. They'll be able to carve it on my tombstone.'

'Not for a good few years yet,' he protested. 'And since you've got plenty of time to change it, what would you *like* it to say?'

'I don't know. Something ... something *interesting*, I suppose.'

What Hubert found interesting was that *she* thought she *wasn't*. He said slowly, 'I reckon that means you want to *do* something interesting. I'll set my mind on it.'

* * *

Through the carriage window and trying not to be obvious about it, Sylvia watched Monsieur Didier riding beside Mr Audley. Both of them were laughing which made her sorry she couldn't hear what they were saying. The Frenchman looked different when he laughed; younger, warmer ... more attractive. And last night, he had stolen her breath by whirling her expertly and so unexpectedly around the floor. Altogether, she thought, she was becoming far too intrigued by Monsieur Didier.

'Watching Mr Audley, are you Syl?' asked Lavinia, following her gaze. 'Can't blame you for that. I can never decide who's the best-looking – him or Lord Nicholas.'

'In my book, Lord Chalfont beats them both,' came the absent reply. 'And I thought we agreed to stop shortening our names?'

'You're getting very particular all of a sudden,' remarked Mrs Hayward tartly. 'All this about *names*, for the Lord's sake! When all's said and done, what does it matter?'

'It matters to me.' Sylvia decided to change the subject before Mama got her teeth into it. 'Caroline says there's a good milliner in the middle of town ... and a decent-sized linen-draper a bit further on. You might find something you like at either one.'

'So might you,' said Lavinia. And added slyly, 'Unless you're shopping for summat else?'

'Don't be daft. But I can visit the shops at home, can't I? So today, I'm going to see the castle with Lady Chalfont and the children. I reckon it'll be fun.'

What was definitely *not* fun was the gusty wind blowing off the sea which promptly sent Julian's hat bowling down the street with Tom and Rob in hot pursuit.

'Dear me,' drawled Rockliffe, tucking Adeline's hand securely through his arm. 'Bracing does not entirely describe this, does it?'

'It is a *little* wild,' she admitted, gazing out on white-capped waves, 'but a wonderful excuse for cuddling up to one's husband.'

'Do you need an excuse? I hadn't noticed.'

Gathering the party together, Bertrand said, 'You are all at liberty to spend the next two hours as you wish. The sea-front promenade is before you, the centre of town lies down that street to our left and those wishing to visit the castle should follow me. We shall meet for luncheon at the coaching inn across the road.'

Mrs Hayward and Lavinia immediately set off in the direction of the shops. Rockliffe and Adeline, together with Lord and Lady Amberley, and followed at a little distance by Mr Maitland and Lady Brassington, decided to brave the elements with a stroll along the sea-front. Everyone else followed Bertrand.

'Are you *sure* there won't be knights in armour?' Ellie asked for perhaps the tenth time. 'Or even a princess? All castles have a princess, don't they?'

'Not this one, apparently.' Arabella looked down at the child and decided to grasp the nettle. 'Ellie … I know you're angry with Tom because he wouldn't do what you asked him to. But I don't think you properly understand what I told you about Christmas wishes. I didn't promise they *would* come true. I just said they *might*.'

'I know. But if lots of people all wish for the same thing --'

'That isn't how it works.'

'How do you know?' argued Ellie before coming to a sudden halt as the castle came into view. 'Oh. I thought it would be bigger and square with high walls – but it's not like that at all. Why is it round?'

'I don't know. You'll have to ask Bertrand.'

Ellie nodded and ran off. Catching up with Julian, Arabella said, 'I've tried to make her see that she's wishing for the moon but she won't listen – so it's your turn.'

'What makes you think she'll listen to me?'

'Because she always does. She thinks the sun shines out of you.'

Julian looked at her, his expression mildly hurt. 'And you don't?'

Arabella laughed. 'Oh yes. I do. I'm just not always sure which bit of you it shines out *of*. And don't try to distract me because it won't work. Tomorrow is Christmas Eve – so talk to Ellie, please. Today.'

The party collected on the bridge traversing the castle ditch while Bertrand hammered on the heavy oak door. Finding Tom beside her, Sylvia said hesitantly, 'That took a lot of courage – what you did last night.'

He shoved his hands in his pockets and huffed an impatient breath.

'I don't mean to be rude – but I wish everybody'd stop staying that. It wasn't about me. It was about Sir Julian and what kind of man he is.'

'And you made that clear enough. But what you said about him said something about you as well.' She smiled at him. 'What does your sister want you to wish for?'

'I promised not to say. I expect everybody else she asked did the same – which makes it a pretty stupid sort of secret. But when Ellie gets a bee in her bonnet ...' He shrugged. 'All I can tell you is that it'll take more than wishing.'

The big double doors swung open, revealing a red-coated sergeant who exchanged a few words with Monsieur Didier before beckoning his visitors into a wide, vaulted space, lit by torches. Then, when everyone was assembled, he said, 'Welcome to Deal Castle, ladies and gentlemen – built by King Henry the Eighth over two centuries ago as a part of his coastal defences. I'm Sergeant Flint and you'll find half a dozen of my troopers scattered about the castle. If you've got questions, they'll try to answer 'em. You can go anywhere you like except the Captain's lodging – not as you *can* go there because as he's not here so it's locked – and stay off all the parapets. Picking bodies out of the moat or mopping up blood from the lower bastions is a nuisance.' He winked at Rob. 'Now, there's eight fully working culverins about the place. Get as close as you like but don't climb on 'em, young sirs. If you want to know how they're loaded and fired, the troopers will explain but don't expect a practical demonstration. We can't have the town in a panic thinking the French have invaded – ah, no offence Mr Didier.'

'None taken,' murmured Bertrand. 'Lord Sarre sends his thanks, by the way, for allowing us to visit today.'

'Our pleasure, sir. Visitors make a welcome change. So feel free to explore, ladies and gentlemen. The castle is yours.'

Tom and Rob instantly dashed for the stairs leading downwards. With a lazy wave of his hand, Mr Audley set off in their wake, saying, 'If there's a dungeon, can I lock them in, Belle?'

'By all means – as long as you let them out in time for luncheon.'

'Be careful they don't lock *you* in one,' grinned Nicholas, preparing to follow him. Then, 'Coming, Ellie?'

'No. There might be skeletons.' She grasped Julian's hand. 'I'll stay with you.'

'Good idea,' said Arabella, giving her husband a meaningful glance. And to the other ladies, 'Which way? Up and work our way down – or the other way about?'

Sylvia got her first proper sight of the castle's structure when she emerged on the roof of the keep with Lady Chalfont, Lady Nicholas and Mistress Audley. She walked slowly around the perimeter, its centre crowned with a lantern, and looked down on the inner and outer bastions, marvelling at how pretty they were ... two tiers of semi-circular petals, the lower one larger than the upper and the whole surrounded by a grassy ditch. Sylvia had seen drawings of castles in books but none that had looked like this one which, to her, resembled a fancy cake. Below her, she could see Tom and Rob learning about one of the big guns from a trooper. Nearby, the other ladies laughed and chattered with each other. Sylvia wished they would go away so she could enjoy it with only the screaming gulls and the sound of miles of empty grey sea for company.

It was over an hour later when the party was starting to gather downstairs and Bertrand judged them almost ready to leave that he realised one of their number was missing. He said, 'Does anyone know where Mademoiselle Sylvie is?'

Heads were shaken and Cassie said, 'She was with Madeleine and me a little while ago but I didn't notice her leaving us.'

'She went up to the top,' offered Tom. 'She passed Rob and me on the stairs a bit ago. Shall I go and fetch her?'

Bertrand shook his head. 'No. I'll find her. If anyone wishes to explore the town or seek a warm fire, you need not wait. And there will be luncheon at the King's Head in an hour.'

He ran up the two flights of stone stairs and emerged into the light and stiff breeze of the upper level. And there was Sylvia, seemingly intent on trying to pick up one of the cannon balls stacked in a neat pyramid beside a culverin. Bertrand spent a few moments watching her struggle with her billowing cloak, the hair falling into her eyes and the slipperiness of the ball against her gloved fingers. He almost laughed. Instead, strolling towards her, he said, 'Sergeant Flint can arrest you for that.'

She had just managed to get a grip on the topmost ball but his words took her by surprise and caused her to fumble. The ball escaped, bounced down the rest of the stack ... and rolled merrily away. Sylvia shot upright, looking horrified and shouted, 'Catch it! Stop it before it goes down one of the --'

Bertrand hurled himself across the intervening space and managed to trap the ball with his foot roughly six inches from one of several drainage holes. Along with a sigh of relief, Sylvia muttered, 'That was your fault.'

He picked up the ball, grunting at the surprising weight of it, and turned, raising satiric brows. 'My fault? How so?'

'You startled me – creeping up like that.'

'Creeping? I don't think so. And you nearly sent the whole pile rolling.'

'Nearly – but didn't.'

'No. You were lucky.' Bertrand bent to put the ball back in its place. 'Out of interest, why were you trying to pick it up?'

'For the sake of it? To see how heavy it is? I don't know. I just ...' She stopped.

'Just what?'

She shrugged, looking suddenly uncomfortable. 'I like it up here. And the cannon balls look so round and smooth that I couldn't resist touching them. Sounds stupid, doesn't it?'

'No more so than Tom wanting to stick his arm down the barrel of a culverin.'

'Tom's thirteen. I'm not.'

'No.' He found himself resisting the impulse to tuck a long, ebony curl behind her ear and said, 'But not so *very* much older, I think. Where is your hat?'

'In a room downstairs. It was a nuisance.' Something in his gaze ... some quality she couldn't identify ... invited confidence. Without stopping to think, she blurted, 'I waited till everybody had gone back down so I could have this all to myself for a bit.' He nodded, as if he found this perfectly reasonable but said nothing. So she continued jerkily, 'Mama and Lavinia talk. All the time. So sometimes I want ... I need ...'

'Quiet,' supplied Bertrand. 'Of course. The others have gone on ahead. If you wish, I could wait for you downstairs.' She said nothing, only looked at him with a sort of surprised uncertainty. This time, he didn't stop himself tucking that fluttering curl away and when she still said nothing, murmured, 'Or I could stay and ... *not* talk.'

An odd little quiver rippled through Sylvia's chest. Did he mean that literally ... or did he mean something else? The realisation that, if he *did* mean something else she wouldn't mind, struck without warning. So she whispered, 'Stay.' And waited.

It was Bertrand's turn to be surprised. On the previous evening, he had finally admitted to himself that he was irresistibly drawn to Sylvia Hayward; that something about her called to him in a way no other girl ever had. The possibility that it might be mutual had not occurred to him. It did so now, providing a moment of temptation. But aware that, if he was mistaken, acting upon it would embarrass both of them, he stepped back and made a slight bow but said nothing. For a second, he thought he glimpsed disappointment in her eyes but she turned away before he could be sure. Then she said abruptly, 'I suppose we *should* join the others.'

'When you are ready. A few minutes more will not matter.'

'No,' said Sylvia, annoyed with herself because not minding if he kissed her was a vastly different thing from wishing he had. She'd thought that asking him to stay had been a big enough hint but apparently not. Unless he didn't *want* to kiss her? Or – and here a huge and unexpected possibility occurred to her – he was too gentlemanly to take advantage. Before she could stop herself, she said, 'Why did you dance with me last night?'

He gave an almost imperceptible shrug.

'Because the opportunity presented itself?'

'That's no answer. Why *me*?'

The truth was that he hadn't thought about it, not even for a second. Even with everything that had been going on and in a room full of people, he had been intensely aware of her throughout the entire evening. So he'd acted purely on impulse, knowing that someone – probably Sebastian Audley – would rib him about it later. And now she was asking for a reason and all he had was a truth he would prefer not to share.

He said, 'It isn't very complicated. I wanted to.'

Sylvia blinked. 'You mean you wanted …?'

'To dance with you. Yes. And now we have settled that point – and it appears you no longer want quiet – we should re-join the other guests before someone sends out a search party.' He offered his arm. 'Shall we?'

Repressing a sigh, she laid her hand on his sleeve, walked with him to the stairs and preceded him down them. She could usually tell when a man was interested in her – not that there had been many since most of the ones she met gravitated towards Lavinia. But Bertrand Didier was different … which she supposed was what she liked about him but which also made him hard to fathom.

At the bottom of the first flight of stairs, her mind still busy with possibilities, she turned aside to collect her hat and then gave an unlovely shriek as something shot past her foot.

'*Aargh*!' She leapt backwards, cannoning into Bertrand. '*A rat*!'

Knocked off balance, his hands automatically gripped her shoulders while his eyes raked the room. He hadn't seen whatever had alarmed her but was fairly sure that if it *had* been a rat he would have done. He said, 'Unlikely, I would think.'

Sylvia turned, burying her face in his shoulder and achieving a stranglehold on his neck. 'It was! I hate them. G-Get *rid* of it!'

Bertrand might have laughed or even suspected a stratagem had she not been shaking. But since she was, he was by no means averse to putting his arms around her and saying gently, 'It was probably just a mouse, Sylvie – and it has gone. See?'

She shook her head and held on tight. 'I can't. They t-terrify me. Always have. Years ago, one got into the kitchen and ...' She stopped, shuddering. 'I can't look.'

'All right. Move with me while I do.' Since her grip didn't allow him to turn his head, he revolved in a slow circle, taking her with him. 'There's nothing here.'

'You're sure?'

'*Absolument*. Quite, quite sure.'

Sucking in a breath and lifting her head, Sylvia took a cautious glance around. 'Oh.' Her fingers relaxed their hold on him but didn't let go. 'You don't think it might come back?'

'No.' He didn't think it had ever been there in the first place but had no objection to continuing to hold her so he said, 'But if it does, I shall frighten it away again.' And then, giving way to temptation, brushed a light, fleeting kiss over her lips.

At least, light and fleeting had been his intention until her eyes fluttered shut, a sighing breath fanned his cheek and she tilted her head in an invitation he found himself incapable of refusing. So he gathered her more comfortably into his arms, slid a hand up into her hair and sought her mouth again. She made a tiny involuntary sound and her lips parted ... and he lost the ability to think.

Sylvia had been kissed precisely twice before and found neither occasion momentous. This was different. Bertrand's mouth asked and hers answered. It was as if they had done this before many times; as if, in some magical way, they recognised each other from another place and time ... the scent and taste of him at once both familiar and a fast-burning fuse.

It was Sergeant Flint's voice calling an order to one of the troopers that brought Bertrand to his senses. He broke the kiss but continued to hold her, looking into her face and waiting until she opened her eyes. Then she did ... and what he saw in them dazzled him. Wonder, delight ... and the same bone-deep sense of *rightness* that he himself felt.

He forced himself to let her go, stepping back to create some necessary space between them. Dimly, he realised that he ought to say something, probably an apology. He hauled in a breath and prepared to do his best. But before he could get a word out, Sylvia floored him with a wide, sweet smile and said, 'Don't.'

'Don't what, *cherie*?' The endearment slipped out before he could stop it.

'Don't say you're sorry. You're not, are you?'

'No ... though I am aware that I ought to be.'

'Why? If *you* should, then so should I.'

He shook his head, half amused and half surprised.

'That is not how it works. A gentleman takes the blame.'

'That's nonsense. Blame doesn't come into it.' She laid her palm briefly against his cheek. 'You didn't do anything I didn't want and – and it was lovely. Please don't spoil it.'

It occurred to Bertrand that, unlike a good many young ladies, Sylvia didn't seem to be expecting a declaration of some kind. Although, with his brain still not fully functional, this was a relief, he couldn't help wondering *why* she didn't. But since this wasn't the moment to investigate either his feelings or hers, he took her hand to drop a light kiss on her knuckles and said, 'Spoiling it is the last thing I wish to do and would, in any event, be impossible. But if we don't want to be asked awkward questions, we really must join the others. We've already been away too long.'

'Oh don't worry about that,' she laughed. 'When I tell them about the rat, Mama and Lavinia won't give it a second thought. They'll just sympathise with you for being stuck with the job of stopping me screaming.'

On the short walk to the King's Head, with her hand tucked firmly in Bertrand's arm and his free hand covering it, Sylvia wondered what had just happened and whether he had felt it too. She thought he had. She wished she dared ask but knew she must not. Casting a quick sideways glance at him, she discovered that he was looking at her ... and was immediately trapped by his gaze and the unexpected discovery that it held a faint smile.

For perhaps the space of five heartbeats, there was silence between them.

Then, as if answering an unspoken question, Bertrand said simply, 'Yes.'

CHAPTER SEVEN

With perfect timing, the snow arrived overnight so that everyone arose on Christmas Eve to a light, pristine covering of white on the far side of the windows.

The children, inevitably, were wildly excited – from Vanessa Jane to Tom, though the latter was naturally careful not to show it. Rob regretted that there wasn't enough for snowballs or snowmen but, optimistic as ever, hoped more might arrive later.

Over breakfast, Adrian announced that everyone had a busy day ahead.

'Bertrand will be leading the gentlemen and older children on an expedition across the fields to gather festive greenery for everywhere as yet undecorated. I'm sure you'll enjoy yourselves and come back laden with holly and mistletoe for the ladies to transform into kissing boughs and the like.'

'You aren't joining us yourself?' asked Nicholas suspiciously.

'Alas, no,' replied Adrian, sounding far too cheerful. 'Caroline and I are delivering the Yuletide baskets around the estate – a task which I fear will occupy much of the day.'

'You fear correctly,' agreed Caroline. 'Fifty-two houses to visit and something to eat or drink in *all* of them.'

Mr Audley laughed. 'Not sounding the better option now, is it Adrian?'

Lord Sarre contented himself with a quelling look and was about to leave the room when Julian drew him to one side and said, 'While you're visiting the tenants, will you ask if any of them can sell me a baby goat?'

Adrian stared at him and then grinned. 'A kid, Julian. A baby goat is called a kid.'

'Yes, I know. Can you find me one? By tomorrow? I'll pay whatever it costs.'

'Ah. Let me guess. A distraction for Ellie?'

'A last resort,' groaned Julian. 'So will you?'

'I'll do my best. But if all else fails, would a kitten do? We have plenty of those.'

'No. It has to be a goat – and preferably female since, if it ends up living in the house, I'd rather it didn't grow horns.' And when Adrian laughed, he added darkly, 'Yes. You think it's funny *now* … but just wait until Benedict is older and Caroline thinks you can protect him from an inevitable disappointment. *Then* you'll know.'

* * *

In the end, the only gentleman who did *not* join Bertrand's expedition was Mr Maitland, who said he was too old and town-bred for tramping through the countryside. Tom and Rob were ready to set forth at least an hour earlier than necessary. Lord Amberley's small son demanded to go with his papa and was allowed to do so when both his mama and his nurse felt he was sufficiently wrapped up. This immediately led to Vanessa demanding to go with *her* papa – which resulted in Rockliffe (who'd had every intention of enjoying a tranquil hour in the library) finally agreeing, for the sake of everyone's peace, to take her. And Ellie, who had been half-inclined to stay behind hunting for fairies, eventually decided that Julian needed her more and set off with the rest, skipping along at his side.

Watching through the drawing-room window, Cassie said, 'Just look at them! Hats, scarves, gloves, boots … are we expecting a blizzard?'

'Let's hope not.' Arabella watched Madeleine and Adeline disentangling a heap of ribbons and miscellaneous trimmings. 'Caroline said there are also fruits ready for use in the kitchen – oranges studded with cloves, that sort of thing.'

'And we'll want those later,' said Adeline, 'but while we wait for the greenery to arrive, we'd better start making swags and bows for hanging it.'

'What is in the garden?' asked Madeleine. 'I know everything will be gone to seed or sleeping for the winter but some things may be pretty; evergreen shrubs or herbs – particularly rosemary, if we're to make a kissing boughs. And the walled garden at Devereux House was looking surprisingly colourful when we --'

'That's it!' said Cassie. 'We need the gardener – Mr Bailes, is it? Caroline says he's a wonder. He'll know what is suitable and probably supply it as well. Shall we send a groom to fetch him?'

'Would it not be simpler for us to go to him?' asked Adeline. 'Madeleine – you're the most artistic one among us. Why don't you and I go? I'd suggest Lily except that she has mysteriously vanished.'

'That's no mystery,' grinned Arabella. 'Mr Maitland's still in the house, isn't he?'

This caused a ripple of laughter into which Cassie said, 'They *do* seem to have become very close ... though it's hard to imagine anything coming of it after they leave here.'

'Sad but true,' agreed Madeleine, coming to her feet. 'And after yesterday I am more interested in what may be going on between Sylvie Hayward and Bertrand.'

Adeline looked up. 'Nothing, surely? Mrs Hayward held forth about Sylvia's terror of rats until I was squirming. Not that I saw any sign of one while we were there.'

'None of us did. Odd, isn't it? But not as odd as Bertrand's reticence on the subject. The one thing on which one can *always* rely is that sly sense of humour of his ... which yesterday was inexplicably absent.' Madeleine smiled and shrugged. 'So let us go to Devereux House and pay a call on Mademoiselle Sylvie.'

* * *

In a corner of the library, Hubert was surprised to find himself losing to Lily at *ecarté*. After the third disastrous game, he sat back in his chair and said, 'You're a dark horse, aren't you? Will you wipe the floor with me at cribbage as well?'

She shook her head, laughing a little. 'Why? Were you going to suggest a game?'

'I was thinking of it. But I reckon we'll carry on playing for shillings.'

'We will indeed. No sane person plays for more than they can afford to lose.'

He scooped up the cards and shuffled them absent-mindedly. Not for the first time, he wondered precisely *how* careful she had to be with money. He said, 'Who do you usually play with?'

'Like-minded souls. There are a few, you know – even in London. And you?'

'A couple of old codgers I've known for years and Caroline when she came to visit. But I don't play very often these days. That's why it's been a pleasure battling the duke over a few hands of piquet.' He smiled at her across the table. 'And now there's you, my lady. I always enjoy a surprise.'

She smiled back but said, 'I was Lily, was I not?'

'You were. You still are.' His hands continued toying with the cards. Then, before he could think better of it, he said, 'Have you never thought of marrying again?'

'There has been no occasion to think of it. No one has ever offered.'

'*What*?' The cards fell in a heap. 'A fine-looking woman, widowed for years … and none of these fancy London gentlemen ever *asked*? What's the matter with them?'

He was so clearly flabbergasted that she couldn't help laughing.

'Are you sure that is the right question?'

'*Da – completely* sure!'

'Oh. Well … thank you. That is very flattering. But really --'

'It's not flattering and there's only one 'but' as far as I can see.' Hubert gathered the cards and started to deal before something escaped from his mouth without first spending sufficient time in his brain. 'If all the men you know are either blind or stupid, you're best off without 'em.'

* * *

'I suppose,' said Mrs Hayward huffily, 'our Caro couldn't be bothered coming herself. Better things to do than take tea with her mother, I daresay.'

'She and his lordship are busy distributing the usual Yuletide gifts to the tenants,' returned Adeline coolly. 'However, I understand that you will all be joining us later --'

'Oh aye. When she's done playing Lady Bountiful and it suits her. Never thought I'd see the day when Caro thought herself too good for us and --'

'*Mam*!' Lavinia was usually immune to undercurrents but even she could see the frost forming in the duchess's aquamarine eyes. 'Forget about Caro. It's lovely of *her Grace* to call on us, isn't it?'

Adeline heard the emphasis and wondered whether the girl was reminding her mother that she was talking to a duchess or how that duchess should properly be addressed.

'Well, of course.' Mrs Hayward managed a smile and something resembling a curtsy. 'It's always a pleasure to see you, your Grace. That goes without saying.'

'Apparently so,' agreed Adeline, sweetly.

Hiding a smile, Madeleine ended what promised to become a yawning silence.

'In fact, the duchess and I need a word with Mr Bailes. I took the liberty of asking Mrs Clayton if --'

'Bailes? Who's he when he's at home?'

'He's the gardener, Mam,' whispered Lavinia. 'You met him t'other day.'

'Oh. Him. Well, no doubt he's somewhere about. Go and order tea, Lavvy – and tell the housekeeper to send some of my plum cake along with it.'

'Please don't trouble, Miss Hayward.' Adeline had heard all about the infamous plum cake from Adrian. 'Unfortunately, Lady Nicholas and I must return to Sarre Park as soon as we have consulted with Mr Bailes. Another day, perhaps?'

It was fortunate that the door opened on Sylvia, thus sending her mother's thoughts in a different direction. 'And where have *you* been all morning, Miss? Sitting with your nose in a book again? Lord knows what good you think that will be in finding a husband because if gentlemen like clever women, I've never seen any sign of it.'

'Yes, Mama. So you've told me.' With a neat curtsy, Sylvia said, 'Your Grace, Lady Nicholas ... Mrs Clayton said to tell you Mr Bailes is waiting in the walled garden so you can see what there is that might suit. Shall – shall I show you the way?'

Madeleine knew the way perfectly well but she said, 'Please do. You must excuse us, Mrs Hayward. But as the duchess has said, we shall see you later for the wassailing.'

As they left the room, Adeline said pleasantly, 'You enjoy reading, Sylvia?'

'Yes – and I've the chance to do it here. At home, there are hardly any books and Mama thinks reading anything except the fashion periodicals and the society pages is a waste of time.'

'I should not say this,' remarked Adeline calmly, 'but she is mistaken about that – and equally mistaken in thinking that gentlemen don't care for intelligent ladies. They do ... if, that is, they are remotely intelligent themselves. So carry on reading, my dear. And if you run out of books, ask Caroline or Adrian for more.' Then, stepping out into the garden, 'Mr Bailes – thank you for sparing us some of your time. I hope we find you well?'

Leaving Adeline to outline their mission to the gardener, Madeleine smiled at Sylvia and said, 'Have you recovered from yesterday's fright?'

'Oh yes.' Sylvia's colour rose a little and she tumbled into speech. 'I feel stupid about it now. I was *sure* it was a rat but Monsieur Didier didn't think it had been – though he was very kind and didn't laugh at me.'

'No? Then you were lucky. Bertrand usually laughs at *everyone* – even me. But then, I have known him since long before Adrian married your sister.'

'Oh. I didn't know. I suppose … naturally he'd be different with old friends.'

'Of which you are not one,' nodded Madeline. And with a lift of her brows, 'But perhaps a new one?'

Her colour rising still further, Sylvia opened her mouth, closed it again and finally said, 'Perhaps. Yes. I'd like to think so.'

Madeleine smiled at her, nodded again and – having found out what she wanted to know – joined in Adeline's discussion with Mr Bailes about pairing bay with ivy.

* * *

Despite the cold, there was a good deal of raillery and laugher amongst the foraging party. The first to find some mistletoe, Mr Audley made instant use of it to claim a kiss from both Ellie and Vanessa, making both of them giggle. Lord Amberley lifted his small son up to tug at bits of ivy and Nicholas hoisted Rob aloft to cut otherwise unreachable branches of holly. Bertrand and Tom took on the task of cutting boughs of pine with the shears; and Julian resigned himself to dragging one of the barrows in which the various cuttings were being piled. Rockliffe, with his small daughter perched on his arm, towed the other.

When the initially intermittent flurries of snow turned heavier, everyone agreed that they had sufficient greenery to decorate Windsor Castle and set off back to the house. The homeward trek began decorously enough until Bertrand and Sebastian started a snowball fight with Tom and Rob … during which virtually everyone else was struck by supposedly misaimed balls. Nicholas got one in the back of his neck; Lord Amberley took one full in the face; and Julian was left brushing wet snow from a part of his anatomy no gentleman wanted attracting attention.

The party surged in on a tide of cold air with tingling fingers and pink noses. Gratefully, Rockliffe and Amberley handed their children over to the nursery-maids and everyone else came in stamping snow from their feet. Arabella and Cassie scolded them about the latter, admired the extent of their haul and then sent them off to change their wet clothes before gathering in the dining room where hot soup would be waiting.

'Where is Madeleine?' Nicholas asked.

'She went to Devereux House with Adeline,' replied Cassie.

'What on earth for?'

'To look for herbs and dried foliage from the garden.' Aware that Bertrand was within earshot, she added innocently, 'And to ask if Miss Sylvia had recovered from yesterday.'

Bertrand turned slowly but before he could speak, Nicholas said, 'I imagine that depends on whether or not her mother is still blathering on about rats. That woman has the sensitivity of a cabbage.'

'She certainly can't take a hint,' agreed Arabella, 'because I dropped at least three.'

'Which everyone noticed except Mrs Hayward,' grinned Nicholas. 'Just out of interest, Bertrand ... *was* there a rat?'

'No. But she thought there was, so the result was the same.'

'Well, if her hysterics prompted her to hurl herself on your manly chest, I hope you took a few moments to enjoy it.'

Bertrand smiled back under raised brows. 'If there's anything at all enjoyable in a girl shaking with fright, you'll have to explain what it is.' And to Cassie, when Nicholas's jaw went slack, 'Is Adrian back yet?'

'No. Caroline sent word that we should not hold luncheon back for them – though with the wassailers due this evening and so much to do before then, I doubt any of us will sit down to eat.' She looked out through the window. 'I'm so glad it has snowed. It makes everything truly festive, doesn't it?'

It also, reflected Bertrand, made sending a carriage out – even over a short distance – a chancy business. But he would do it anyway ... not only because it was unfair to leave the Hayward ladies alone on Christmas Eve or even because he wanted to see Sylvie ... but because if, as seemed possible, tongues were wagging about the two of them, she needed to be made aware of it before her mother was. It would, however, be sensible to send the carriage before dark. And if the weather worsened and the ladies had to remain at Sarre Park overnight, arrangements would simply have to be made.

* * *

The afternoon was a hive of industry, laughter and Christmas cheer.

Below stairs, the household staff was busy getting ready for the invasion of the wassailers. Croft, the butler, sent a pair of footmen to bring in barrels of ale while he himself prepared great quantities of spiced wine. In the kitchens, Lily Brassington rolled up her sleeves, donned an apron and worked alongside Cook, Betsy and two maids to make dozens of small fruit pies, curd tarts and cinnamon-spiced biscuits.

Above stairs, everyone joined in the task of decorating the house with swathes of greenery tied up with red velvet bows and knots of gold ribbon. Madeleine directed operations in between fashioning two kissing balls made of mistletoe, rosemary and variegated ivy threaded through with scarlet braid. The gentlemen hauled in the Yule log and set it ablaze in the fireplace of the great hall; Arabella and Cassie embellished mantelpieces with boughs of pine, red-berried holly and gilded pine-cones; and the children ran hither and thither, growing progressively more excited and getting under everybody's feet.

By the time Adrian and Caroline returned, the house was redolent with the scent of spices and the decorative transformation almost complete. Caroline went from room to room, staring about her in delight. She said, 'It's wonderful! I never imagined you'd be able to do so much ... but *thank* you. It all looks beautiful.'

'The only thing still to be done,' said Adeline, 'is the hanging of the kissing boughs. And we all agreed *that* task should fall to Adrian as host.'

He grinned. 'Does the privilege of the first kisses go with it?'

'That probably depends on who you want to kiss,' remarked Mr Audley.

Recognising the provocation, Caroline smiled kindly and answered in Adrian's stead.

'Don't worry, Sebastian. Even pretty as you are – it won't be you.'

She was rewarded with a gust of laughter, under cover of which Adrian murmured, '*Pretty*, is he?' And aloud, when he could make himself heard, 'Now ... where am I to hang these kissing boughs?'

A chorus of contradictory suggestions answered him but eventually one ball was suspended from the chandelier in the centre of the hall and the other in the drawing-room doorway. Then, having soundly kissed his wife, for which he received a round of applause, Adrian solemnly declared the festive season officially open.

While everyone else was happily occupied, he sauntered over to Julian and said, 'I got what you wanted. She's in the stables, being cared for by one of the grooms. Apparently the mother rejected her so Mary Wendle's eldest girl has been bottle-feeding her and you – or Ellie – will have to continue with that for a week or two.' He grinned at Julian's faintly alarmed expression. 'Don't look so worried. Mary has sent what you'll need, including half a gallon of goat's milk.'

'Oh. Right. Thank you. How much do I owe you?'

'Nothing – though you might want to pay for the milk. As for the kid ... there *is* a price but it isn't money.'

Julian blinked. 'Then what?'

'A concert. Virtually everyone I spoke to today asked if it would be possible to hear the Virtuoso Earl play. So when Joe Wendle learned that the kid was for *you*, he asked if you might pay for it with a few tunes. Will you?'

'Of course. I'd be happy to. But I don't see how --'

'I do. I promised to ask you and … hinted … that you'd probably say yes. So by now word will have gone round and I'll wager we'll have most of the tenants and half the village turning up this evening with the wassailers. I don't know how loud you can make the harpsichord but --'

'Yes you do,' murmured Julian with a shrug. 'Do you remember *La Marche des Scythes*?'

'Unfortunately, I do,' grinned Adrian. And then, 'So with the doors left open, folk could listen from down here in the hall?'

'Yes.'

'Excellent. Then the only thing we need worry about is having room for them all.'

CHAPTER EIGHT

Although the snow had stopped, Bertrand suspected there was more on the way and therefore sent the carriage to Devereux House an hour before the light began to fail. The Hayward ladies arrived at Sarre Park just ahead of a fresh flurry of flakes and were ushered in to thaw out by the fire. Then everyone gathered to enjoy the particularly substantial tea that Caroline had ordered due to the fact that dinner was to be replaced by a buffet supper after the tenants, villagers and wassailers had departed.

Under cover of joking with Tom and Rob, Bertrand watched Sylvia, vibrantly pretty in a pale blue *robe a l'Anglais*. As if feeling his gaze, she glanced his way. Their eyes met and held; a tiny smile, surely meant just for him, curved her lips ... then she turned away to reply to something Cassie said to her.

Since those minutes at Deal Castle, Bertrand had been mentally berating himself for an idiot. He'd lost his head; he shouldn't have kissed her; the feeling that something momentous had happened between them was ridiculous – an aberration. How could it be anything else? After all, he scarcely knew the girl – nor she him. He was merely allowing himself to be overtaken by snow and kissing boughs and an uncommonly pretty face. It wasn't real. It didn't mean anything. Next time he saw her, he would be more sensible.

Well, it had only taken one look at her and a glimpse of that secret smile to put all his own good advice to flight. Something had lurched in his chest and just for a second he had forgotten to breathe. Then, when his brain was working properly again, bringing with it a sort of wry desperation, he thought, *Hell. If this is real ... and if we both feel it ... what am I supposed to do? Her bloody mother is going to have a fit.*

Over by the window, meanwhile, gazing with Caroline into the white-flecked dusk, Adrian murmured, 'Your mother and sisters had better stay tonight. I won't risk them – not to mention coachman, groom and horses – getting stranded half-way.'

'I know. And since they came prepared with overnight bags, I suspect Mama was counting on that,' she replied dryly. 'But they'll have to share the only spare bedchamber fit to use. And though the girls won't mind, Mama will grumble.'

'When doesn't she?'

'True.' She eyed the weather doubtfully. 'I'm more concerned about all the people coming here tonight – a lot of them, walking. We have plenty of food and drink to warm them up but they still have to get home again afterwards.'

Adrian laughed and shook his head. 'Don't think that prospect will keep them at home, love. It won't – not with a personal appearance of the Virtuoso Earl in store.'

On the other side of the room, Julian – who had found a few minutes to visit the stables – was telling Arabella about the baby goat's sad start in life and unexpected needs.

'Kid,' she corrected automatically. 'A baby goat is --'

'A kid. Yes, I know. Why does everyone keep on telling me that? It – *she* – is a funny little thing. Much more engaging than I'd expected. And she's been reared in the kitchen. So I thought perhaps --'

'No,' said Arabella instantly. 'She is *not* taking up residence in the house.'

'Well, not here of course. But at home?'

'*No*, Julian. However tiny and funny and charming she is now ... she is a *goat* and, in time, will be a full-grown one.'

'I realise that.'

'I'm not sure you do. How much do you actually *know* about goats?'

He searched his mind and came up blank. 'Nothing, really.'

'Well, I do. They can climb and jump – which means that they can get anywhere. Chairs, table-tops, beds ... your harpsichord?' She watched him shudder and had to hide a smile. 'Also, they eat literally *anything*, regardless of whether it's edible or not. Curtains and rugs, for example. And you seriously want her to live in the house?'

'Oh. Well, since you put it like that ... I suppose not.' He eyed her doubtfully. 'But what about the bottle-feeding?'

'How difficult can it be? If someone shows Ellie what to do, she'll enjoy doing it. It will make her feel very grown-up and responsible.' She slid her fingers into his. 'The kid was a wonderful idea, Julian. God willing, it will take her mind off the other thing.'

* * *

Villagers and tenants started arriving a little in advance of the so-called wassail party which was actually the church choir, seasonally augmented. Lanterns were left at the door and everyone tried to stamp the snow from their boots before stepping into the light and warmth of the hall. Caroline and Adrian began by greeting each family as it arrived but with more and more folk coming through the door, this swiftly became impossible. Fortunately, everyone from the duke and duchess to Hubert Maitland came down to exchange Christmas greetings with the visitors while the footmen and maids did their best to ensure everyone had food and drink.

By the time the singers arrived, the hall was already crowded but somehow room was made for them and they embarked on a medley of Yuletide favourites. *The Holly and the Ivy* was followed by *God Rest Ye Merry Gentlemen* ... and *I Saw Three Ships* had everyone joining in. Finally, an exquisite four-part setting of *The Coventry Carol* caused Julian, leaning against the bannister half-way up the stairs, to listen with closed eyes. And inevitably, a rousing chorus of *The Gloucestershire Wassail* bade fair to raise the roof.

Yet more people arrived, increasing the crush in the hall and causing Rockliffe and Nicholas to usher their pregnant wives, along with Cassie and Rosalind, to the chairs which had been placed for them on the half-landing.

Sylvia saw that Caroline, Arabella and Lily Brassington were carrying around trays of warm mince pies and tarts and that Bertrand was now assisting the servants with pitchers of ale and mulled wine. Leaving her mother and sister standing awkwardly in a corner, she winnowed her way to Caroline's side and, barely managing to make herself heard, said, 'Can I help?'

'Oh *please*!' groaned Caroline gratefully, shoving a basket of cinnamon biscuits into her hands. 'Try to get to the new arrivals – some of them can't get past the porch.'

Sylvia nodded and set off, chatting cheerfully to this or that one as she went. Near the door, her path crossed with Bertrand's and he said rapidly, 'Give those to me, Sylvie. If you go outside your slippers will be soaked.'

Stupidly warmed by his use of her name, she handed him the basket and, not quite brave enough to touch his hair, reached out to brush a few flakes of snow from his shoulders, saying, 'There are people out there?'

'Twenty or thirty and more still arriving. Will you --' He stopped to grab a passing footman, 'Thomas – mugs of hot wine for the crowd outside and make it quick.'

Thomas nodded and dived back through the throng.

Sylvia waited for Bertrand to finish what he had been saying and when he merely stood looking at her, prompted helpfully, 'Will I what?'

He blinked. 'Ah. Yes. Ask Adrian to have Julian start playing before the people who can't get inside freeze.'

Locating her brother-in-law in the crush wasn't easy but she eventually managed it and passed on Bertrand's message. Adrian muttered something under his breath, thanked her and headed up the stairs. Julian was already sitting coatless at the harpsichord doing mysterious things with its settings. Crossing to a window and pulling back the curtains, Adrian said, 'You'd better come and see this.'

Julian rose to join him, took one look and said, 'Oh.'

On the snow-covered gravel below stood a crowd of villagers … some holding lanterns, others stamping their feet and breathing life into their frozen fingers … but all looking cheerfully expectant.

'Why are they there?'

'Because the hall's already packed to the rafters. I'd expected most of the tenants and roughly half the village but --'

Julian didn't wait for him to finish. Throwing the casement wide and moving on to the next, he said, 'Then we'll open the windows. All of them.'

'Are you sure? In less than five minutes it will be perishing in here - _'

'They're standing in the *snow*, Adrian. If they want to hear me play, they're bloody well *going* to.' Having opened the last window, he leaned out and called, 'Good evening, ladies and gentlemen – and a very merry Christmas to you. I'm Julian Langham. Are you waiting for me, by any chance?'

Over a scattering of mingled applause and laughter, someone shouted, 'Aye, m'lord – there being no room at the inn, as it were.'

'Then I'll take a request. Something just for you while Lord Sarre quietens things downstairs.' A glance told him that Adrian had already left the room. 'What shall it be?'

Voices conferred and one of them called, 'A jig'd be good, sir – if you do know one.'

'I do indeed.' And with a grin, 'But if I play it, you must all dance.'

'And *you*, young man,' came a motherly interjection, 'had better put your coat on!'

Julian laughed. 'Yes, ma'am. For once, I fully intend to.'

And thus the recital began.

Lively dance tunes were followed by pieces of Bach, interspersed with Couperin and Scarlatti; then a brief medley of popular songs … followed by more Bach and Mozart, sometimes bright and triumphant, sometimes heart-wrenchingly poignant. And throughout it all, both the audience outside and the one in the hall, listened in awed pleasure.

It was when Julian embarked on the hauntingly lovely Johann Christian Bach *Andante* that Bertrand abandoned his duties in favour of seeking out Sylvia and, eventually finding her, drew her into the only semi-secluded spot he could find. Neither of them spoke; but his arm somehow found its way around her waist and her head came to rest on his shoulder. It seemed both not very much ... yet natural, right and, in this moment, enough.

When the piece ended in the seconds of pure silence that it always produced before the applause rang out, she smiled up at him and said simply, 'That was beautiful. Thank you for listening to it with me.'

He shook his head, gripped by something he could neither name nor understand. Then, because her words left him only one thing to add, he whispered, 'Merry Christmas, Sylvie.' And dropped a fleeting kiss on her brow.

'*Sylvia Hayward*! What are you *doing?*'

The furious – and as usual, far too loud – voice made them both jump and caused several heads to turn. Oddly, however, Bertrand's arm remained where it was and Sylvia made no attempt to move away. She said calmly, 'Lower your voice, Mama – unless you *want* everyone looking?'

Mrs Hayward grabbed her arm and pulled. 'You come with me. Now.'

Sylvia twisted herself free as the first notes of something crisp and pretty rippled down from above. 'Come where? Everybody's jammed in like herrings and not likely to move any time soon, neither.'

'Well, *you* can move, Miss! Right now – and right away from *him*.'

More heads turned and three people hissed at Mrs Hayward to shush. She coloured, pressed her lips together and remained where she was, glaring at Bertrand. He raised a provocative brow and smiled ... fairly sure she was grinding her teeth.

The recital continued for perhaps another ten minutes and concluded with a flourish as Julian treated his audience to Royer's *Le Vertigo*. Having been told that this would be the final piece, Adrian fought his way up the stairs as far as the half-landing and, when the applause and cheering began to die down, held up a hand for silence.

'I don't need to ask if you've enjoyed the concert, ladies and gentlemen ... but Mr Langham will join us presently if you want to thank him in person. Give him a chance to warm up, though. He's been playing with the windows wide open for the benefit of the folk who couldn't squeeze into the house.'

The murmur of surprise which ran through the audience turned to laughter when Arabella said she hoped he'd had the sense to keep his coat on. Then Julian emerged at the top of the stairs to renewed applause, smiled diffidently, and bowed, hand on heart, causing a collective female sigh.

Still holding Sylvia and Bertrand trapped in their shadowy corner, Mrs Hayward renewed her attack. 'What's the *matter* with you, Syl? Come away this minute! Out of all the men you might take a fancy to, why choose a nobody like him?'

Aware that they were now attracting attention, Sylvia stepped out of Bertrand's hold and, her expression hardening, said, 'He is *not* a nobody, Mama – not to me nor to anybody except you. And you've no business talking to him that way.'

'Thank you,' murmured Bertrand. 'But I can speak for myself, you know.'

Ignoring him and before Sylvia had a chance to reply, Mrs Hayward snapped, 'What's going on between the two of you? And how long have you been at it?'

'We are not 'at' anything,' he sighed. 'As for what is going on ... that is yet to be determined. Sylvie?'

She nodded. 'Yes. I don't know either. But I'd like ... I think I'd like to find out.'

With an elegant and extremely Gallic gesture, he took her hand and kissed it.

'*Moi aussi, cherie.* So would I.'

'You can stop right there!' Yet again Mrs Hayward forgot about keeping her voice down. 'There'll be no finding out. I won't have it. You can look higher than *him* for a husband, my girl and --'

'*What?*' Sylvia gaped at her. 'Where did that come from? Nobody that I know of has mentioned marriage – nor even thought of it.'

'I'll wager *he's* thought of it. You've a dowry and connections and he knows it. But I'll be damned before I let you throw yourself away on a – a *servant*!'

'That will do, madam.'

She spun round to find herself facing Lord Sarre, his eyes cold and his tone colder. Unwisely, she opened her mouth only to be cut off before she could utter a sound.

'Not another word. You are embarrassing both my guests and yourself. If you have something to say you may say it in private and with some attempt at civility.'

'Adrian?' Arriving at his side, Caroline looked anxiously from his face to her mother's. 'What is happening?'

'A small fracas. I'll explain later. But, for now, I'll deal with it while you remain with our guests.' He glanced to where Julian was surrounded by admiring girls and men wanting to shake his hand. 'By the look of things, no one is going home just yet. Bertrand, Sylvia ... Mrs Hayward? The library. Now, if you please.'

Caroline frowned, watching them go and then turned to find Lily at her elbow. She said, 'Is there something between Bertrand and Sylvia I don't know about?'

'It rather looks that way, doesn't it?'

'God help Adrian, then. Mama will have a full-blown tantrum.'

Upstairs, and shutting the library door with a snap, Lord Sarre swung round and bade everyone be seated. Sylvia, staring transfixed at the books lining the walls, sat a decorous distance from Bertrand on a sofa. Hovering beside a chair, Mrs Hayward scowled at them and opened her mouth to speak.

'Sit *down*, ma'am,' ordered Adrian again. And when she had very reluctantly done so, 'Let me begin by explaining something to you. Bertrand is my oldest and most trusted friend. What he is *not* – and never has been – is a servant. Consequently, if you cannot treat him with at least an appearance of courtesy whilst under my roof, you will find yourself no longer welcome here. Do I make myself clear?'

She stared at him speechlessly for a full minute. Finally, she said huffily, 'I reckon our Caro will have something to say --'

'*Do I make myself clear?*'

This time her jaw dropped. 'Yes. But --'

'Excellent. Then we will have an end to this nonsense.'

'But not being a servant don't make him a gentleman,' she finished stubbornly.

Adrian impaled her on a withering stare.

'Neither do birth and breeding, ma'am. Manners do that ... a fact of which you, it seems, are lamentably unaware.'

Bertrand, who had been holding his tongue quite successfully thus far, turned a snort of laughter into a cough as he watched Mrs Hayward slowly understand the insult.

Adrian shot him a quelling glance and, softening his tone, said, 'Sylvia ... I don't need to ask this but, for the sake of your mother, I will.

Has Bertrand trifled with your affections or compromised you in any way?'

'No. Of course he hasn't.' She cast a thoroughly irritable glance at her mother. 'Though if he *had*, I could have put a stop to it fast enough – *if*, that is, I'd a mind to.'

'He *kissed* you!' shouted Mrs Hayward. 'I saw him do it. What's more, he had his arm round you as if you was --'

'We listened to Mr Langham's music and Bertrand wished me a merry Christmas. What's wrong with that? A kiss on the forehead in a room full of people --'

'And any number of 'em could've seen what I saw,' pronounced her mother triumphantly. 'Do you *want* folk taking you for a lightskirt?'

'That is enough, I think.' Deciding that it was time he took a hand in this, Bertrand stood up. 'No sensible person will think Mademoiselle Sylvie anything but an innocent and charming *jeune fille*. But should anyone be misguided enough to speak ill of her, I will be happy to correct their mistake.'

'And *then* what? Offer to do right by her? Yes. That'd be handy for you, wouldn't it?'

'God,' muttered Sylvia disgustedly. 'Take no notice of her, Bertrand. Aside from her jumping to daft conclusions same as always, she's got this crazy notion that Lavinia and I are both going to marry lords.'

'And so you *could*,' insisted Mrs Hayward, 'if only Caro'd put you in the way of meeting a few single, titled gentlemen.'

'No. She could introduce us to a hundred and it still wouldn't work. How many times do I have to say it? Just because Caroline married an earl doesn't mean Lavinia and me can do likewise. We don't have Caroline's education. We don't speak properly; we don't know how to go on in polite company; and we don't know anything about music or books or art. No!' This as her mother was about to interrupt. 'Just *listen* for once. Even if some lord fell head over heels in love with one of us, you can bet he'd draw the line at marriage. Because the truth is that if Mr Maitland hadn't given us an allowance after Papa died, Lavinia and me would've had to earn a living as seamstresses or shop girls. And *that's* what any titled gentleman would see – not our looks or the fact our sister's a countess. They'd see girls their mothers would class as house-maids.' She turned to Adrian and added, 'Tell her I'm right. She might believe it then.'

'I think you give yourself too little credit,' he replied slowly. 'But in essence, yes. What you say is true to a degree. It's the way of the world, I'm afraid.'

'And I don't mind it,' she said firmly. 'I'd rather marry a man I *like* than one I don't particularly just because he's got a title. That's what Caroline did. Anybody can see she married the man first and the earl second.'

'Thank you,' murmured Adrian, amused.

'Fustian!' Mrs Hayward rose in an irritable rustle of magenta taffeta. 'With a dowry of a hundred thousand pounds, I should hope Caroline wouldn't have been ninny enough to settle for a plain mister. But I've had enough of this. Come along, young lady. It's time we joined the rest of the company – and I'll not hear any arguments.'

Sylvia stood up, willing to leave before the situation could get any worse. But before she could take a step, Adrian said, 'A moment, Sylvia. The duchess and Madeleine have informed me in no uncertain terms that I've been remiss in not inviting you to make use of this room. Please feel free to borrow as many books as you wish.'

'May I?' A slight flush touched her cheeks. 'Thank you!'

And then, with a curtsy for Adrian and a brief searching glance at Bertrand, she followed her mother from the room.

As soon as the door closed behind them, Adrian poured two measures of brandy and lapsing into French, said, 'Thank God. That woman has had two husbands. How come neither of them strangled her?'

'It's a mystery,' said Bertrand, accepting the glass he was offered.

'It is.' Adrian resumed his seat and eyed his friend meditatively. 'Do you want to tell me what, if anything, is happening between you and Caroline's sister?'

'Do I have to?'

'No.'

'Good.' Bertrand took a hefty swallow of brandy and muttered, 'I … like her.'

'I'd gathered that much.'

'I think perhaps I might … *more* than like her.'

Adrian nodded encouragingly but said nothing.

'While we were at the castle there was a moment … well, never mind that. Suffice it to say that I think she might like me too.'

'Ah.'

Bertrand stopped staring into his glass and said irritably, 'Is that all you can say?'

'Yes. Having seen first-hand how I conducted my *own* courtship, I assumed you weren't asking for advice.'

Laughter replaced the irritation. 'No. How the hell you got away with that piece of insanity is beyond me.'

'Luck,' grinned Adrian, 'and a bit of help from Mr Bailes. Seriously though … if you and Sylvia want each other, don't let her demented mother get in your way. And if you'd like me to reconsider my intention to pack them off home the day after the ball, you need only say the word.'

CHAPTER NINE

The snow stopped before midnight and Christmas morning dawned chilly but bright, the blanket of white glistening under wintry sunshine. While the rest of the adults gathered in the breakfast parlour, Julian whisked Ellie from the nursery to the stables before she was able to discover that her secret Christmas wish remained unfulfilled. She clapped her hands in delight when she saw the kid and laughed when it pushed her over as she knelt beside it. Inevitably, Julian found himself having to explain that sadly her new pet could not come inside the house but a lesson in bottle-feeding from the young groom detailed to care for the animal made Ellie forget to argue ... and after that came the absorbing question of choosing a name. So when she said she wanted to play with the kid for a little longer Julian heaved a sigh of relief and decided it was probably safe to leave her.

Although the bedchamber problem had been partially solved by Lily Brassington inviting Sylvia to share her room instead of squeezing in with her mother and sister, Mrs Hayward was still shooting darkling glances at Bertrand and Lavinia complained that she'd had hardly a wink of sleep thanks to Mam fidgeting and snoring all night. Everyone else, however, was looking forward to the day ahead and cheerfully discussing plans for it – the first, of course, being church in the village.

'It's not much more than half a mile,' explained Caroline, 'so I thought we might walk? Not the mothers-to-be, of course – Adeline, Madeleine and Cassie must go by carriage. But the rest of us can enjoy a little fresh air and exercise while the snow is still pretty.'

'What she is actually saying,' remarked Adrian, 'is that you *will* walk to church unless you have a verifiable medical condition and a note to prove it.'

* * *

While Tom prised Ellie away from the goat in time to be made tidy for church, everyone else donned hats, cloaks and gloves against the cold and assembled obediently in the hall. Rosalind, her hands buried in a luxurious sable muff, smiled up at her husband and said, 'I love the snow. It reminds me of those days at Oakleigh when we first met and of you bullying me into going outside when I'd been too afraid to try.'

'I did not bully you,' Amberley protested. 'I merely employed my considerable charm to encourage you to come out and play with me.'

'That is certainly *one* way of putting it.'

'You're saying there's another?'

'You put a snowball down my neck!'

'Ah yes. So I did.' He wrapped an arm about her waist. 'And you laughed.'

Pelting down the stairs with her brothers, Ellie skidded to a halt at Rosalind's side and, gazing expectantly up at her, said, 'Merry Christmas, my lady!'

'And a merry Christmas to you too, Ellie. I hear you have a baby goat?'

'Yes. She's called Daisy.' Expectancy turned to uncertainty. 'Did it work?'

Rosalind smiled at her. 'Did what work, darling?'

The sudden, stricken look in the child's eyes caused Amberley's heart to sink. Very cravenly, he'd hoped that this moment would occur when either Julian or Arabella was at hand – which, right now, they weren't. Worse still, Rosalind was the only person in the house who didn't know what Ellie had been up to. He looked helplessly at Rockliffe, his expression one of, *How the hell do I make this, if not better, at least no worse?*

Picking up his cue without so much as a blink, the duke strolled towards Ellie, saying smoothly, 'Do you think *I* might be permitted to see Daisy? I have a particular fondness for goats ... and there is just time now, if we are quick. Come.'

Wordlessly, Ellie allowed him to take her hand and lead her away.

Behind them, Rosalind said blankly, 'Rock likes goats? Since when?'

Amberley touched her cheek with gentle fingers. 'Since he realised I wasn't up to the task of telling Ellie that your sight hasn't miraculously been restored overnight.'

She frowned. 'Why would she think it might have been?'

He drew in a bracing breath and, in as few words as possible, explained.

On their way out of the house, Rockliffe told a completely untruthful tale about a goat he and his siblings had owned as children and, once in the stables, duly admired Daisy whilst dissuading her from chewing his glove. Throughout all of this, Ellie did not say a word. Indeed, he wasn't sure she was even listening. So he sighed and said reflectively, 'Wishes can be strange things, you know. They don't always come true exactly when we want them to ... and rarely in the way we expect.'

Her face pressed against the goat's coarse coat, she muttered, 'You don't have to be nice. I know it didn't work.'

'No. Sadly, it didn't ... just as it has never worked for Lord Amberley. And he's been wishing the same thing, every day for a very long time.'

Tired of being cuddled, Daisy butted Ellie under the chin and danced off.

Sitting back on her heels, she said dully, 'So it was a stupid idea.'

'Far from it. Just because the result isn't the one you hoped for --' He paused as Julian materialised in the doorway looking anxious. 'Ah. Here is your Papa.'

Ellie turned, scrambled up and flew over to throw herself into Julian's arms.

Rockliffe rose, dusted straw from his knee and walked by murmuring, 'You will need a little time, Julian. I'll have a second carriage made ready for you – and explain to Adrian.' Then he was gone.

* * *

Bright-eyed and pink-cheeked from the cold, Lily trod through crisp, shallow snow with her hand firmly tucked into Hubert's arm. She said, 'What would you be doing today if you were at home in Halifax?'

'The early service in the Minster. After that there's always some family or other who invites me to take my dinner with them.' He slanted a smile at her. 'You?'

'Church, of course. Then I spend the rest of the day with a small group of friends, widowed ladies like myself. We take it in turns to play host.' She sighed faintly. 'It is pleasant and companionable. But very sedate and ... well, to be honest, just a little *dull*. Being among so many young people like this is very much livelier.' Lily leaned towards him and lowered her voice. 'And there's romance in the air.'

Hubert's pulse gave a single, unexpected thud. He said cautiously, 'Is there now?'

'Yes. I think Sylvia has developed a *tendre* for Monsieur Didier.'

'Ah.' He tried to decide whether he was relieved or disappointed. 'I take it that means she fancies him?'

'It does. And what is more, I have an idea that her feelings may be reciprocated.'

'Her mother'll have a lot to say about that, then – and none of it good. She still thinks some titled fellow only needs to *see* those girls to be down on one knee before you can blink.' He laughed suddenly. 'As for young Bertrand ... if he and Sylvia want each other, they can likely count on Adrian standing up for them.'

Some little way behind them, Mrs Hayward punctuated her litany of criticism regarding Sylvia's behaviour of the previous evening and the utter unsuitability of Monsieur Didier with complaints that her boots pinched and she was absolutely *not* going to walk back after church. When she fell temporarily silent to catch her breath, Lavinia nudged Sylvia and whispered, 'Is he going to ask you?'

'Ask me what?'

'Don't be dense. He kissed you, didn't he? Is he going to propose? And if he does, will you say yes?'

'Don't be an idiot,' sighed Sylvia. 'Mama's making mountains out of molehills as usual – which is quite annoying enough without you joining in.'

Lavinia pulled a face and opened her mouth to argue but before she could get a word out, her mother said bitterly, 'Just *look* at old man Maitland making a fool of himself with Lady B. I'll bet she laughs herself silly behind his back.'

'She doesn't,' said Sylvia. 'She told me last night that she enjoys his company.'

'Maybe she's set her cap at him,' offered Lavinia.

Mrs Hayward laughed. 'Oh that's likely, isn't it? Giving up her title and going to live cheek-by-jowl with the manufactory in Halifax?'

'She might. From what I've seen, there's not one of her gowns newer than the season before last ... and Mr Maitland's worth thousands, isn't he? If he made her an offer, she'd be mad to turn it down.'

'*If* he did,' her mother sniffed. 'But he won't. Stands to reason he hasn't stayed a widower this long to change his ways now.'

'So how, exactly, is he making a fool of himself?' demanded Sylvia, suddenly losing patience. 'You can't have it both ways, Mama. But nothing pleases you, does it? All you've done since we got here is carp and complain – and I can't be the only one who's getting sick of it. If you can't say something nice for once, why don't you try not saying anything?'

And she stalked away while Mrs Hayward's mouth was still hanging open.

Arriving at the church with Caroline, Adrian came to an abrupt halt at the sight of a plain black chaise standing a short distance from the gate. He knew instantly to whom it belonged. He even realised that he ought to have expected it. But his first thought was, *Oh God. Betsy's right. We're cursed.*

'Adrian?' Caroline touched his arm. 'What is it?'

'Mother,' came the grim reply.

'Oh.'

'Exactly.'

'Well, she is *not* going to spoil our day. I won't have it.' Caroline stiffened her spine. 'We will be beautifully civil ... until she isn't. And we'll pray for a very short sermon.'

The tension faded from Adrian's face. He laughed.

Their own carriages arrived. Rockliffe, Nicholas and Sebastian reclaimed their ladies and when Ellie emerged, still looking doleful and holding Arabella's hand, Amberley guided his wife over to her. Rosalind pulled the child into a warm hug and said, '*Thank* you, Ellie. And please don't be upset. What matters most is that you tried.'

'I wanted you to see John and Deborah,' whispered Ellie. 'I hate it that you can't.'

'I know, darling, and of course I would love to be able to see them. But that you cared enough to do such a kind, unselfish thing ... well, that is a very special Christmas gift that I shall always remember.' Rosalind stood up but retained one of Ellie's hands. 'Now, if your Mama doesn't mind, will you sit with me in church?'

For the first time, the beginnings of a real smile dawned and Ellie nodded vigorously. 'Yes, please. Mama-Belle won't mind at all. And I'd like to.'

Everyone trooped into the church to welcoming smiles from the tenants and villagers who had joined in last night's wassail. And at the front, sitting alone and impossibly straight-backed in the Sarre family pew, was a solitary figure in black figured silk.

'Ah,' said Rockliffe softly to Adrian. 'The Dowager Countess, I presume?'

'Yes ... and overflowing with seasonal good cheer, as usual,' agreed his lordship sardonically. 'Ten guineas says she insists on meeting you after the service.'

'I believe I'll bow to your superior knowledge and decline the wager.' The duke paused, raising his quizzing-glass. 'The veil is a nice touch.'

'Isn't it? And so typically Mother.'

The Dowager did not rise when her son and daughter-in-law entered the pew. She merely nodded regally and said, 'You came.'

'And a merry Christmas to you too, Madam,' responded Adrian, matching his tone to hers. 'Did you suppose we might not?'

'It was a possibility.' Still without acknowledging Caroline, she turned her head briefly to see who had followed them into the church and then looked back at her son to say, 'As was not bringing quite *all* of your guests. But that was clearly too much to hope for.'

Taking her seat and tired of being ignored, Caroline said sweetly, 'And which of them should have been forbidden attendance on this of all days?'

'I am sure you know the answer to that. I have heard, by the way, of last evening's vulgar doings ... something else which might have been better managed.'

'Father spinning in his grave, is he?' asked Adrian. And to Caroline, 'The peasants weren't allowed into the house in his day. They had to tug their forelocks from a respectful distance.'

'Which is as it should be,' snapped the Dowager. '*You*, on the other hand, demean your position at every turn.'

'Well, that must afford you some satisfaction. It's what you always predicted, after all. And you do so enjoy being right.' He met her incensed stare with a cold smile. 'Here come the choir and Reverend Cooper. The service is starting. Hallelujah.'

* * *

As soon as the choir had filed back down the aisle and out into the graveyard, the Dowager Countess rose, replacing her gloves, and said imperiously, 'You may introduce me to some of your guests, Sarre. *Not* the female in the over-trimmed hat who I presume can only be your wife's mother – and not *here*, since I have no wish to linger in the porch being jostled by the tenants --'

'Would any of them dare?' murmured Caroline.

'I was not addressing you, young woman. Pray wait until I do.'

'But don't hold your breath,' advised Adrian. And with a sudden switch to frigid hauteur, 'And *you*, Madam, will either address my wife correctly and with some vestige of civility or there will be no introductions of any kind.'

She glared at him, shrugged and said frostily, 'As you wish.'

'It had better be.'

'As I was saying ... I shall have Fletcher drive me to Sarre Park where I will be pleased to meet Rockliffe and his duchess. Also Lord and Lady Amberley ... and perhaps that odd young earl one reads so much about in the newspapers.'

'That will be a rare treat for them, I'm sure,' he murmured. And before she could speak, 'Are you inviting yourself to dine?'

'No. I imagine that an hour will be quite long enough.' She finished smoothing her gloves and sailed into the aisle. 'For both of us.'

Adrian loosed a breath of pure irritation and turned to Caroline. 'I should have told her to go to the devil, shouldn't I?'

'No.' She tucked her hand through his arm and smiled at him. 'She may be dreadful but she's still your mother. We can manage an hour. But we need to get back quickly.'

It took time to run the gauntlet of smiles and Christmas wishes from the rest of the congregation but as soon as they got outside, Adrian caught up with Julian and said, 'Would you and the family mind walking back?'

'Not in the least. These two,' he grinned at Tom and Rob, 'are itching for a chance to play with the snow. But is there some problem?'

'You could put it that way. Caroline and I need to be home before my bloody mother turns up.' He stopped, glancing at the boys and said, 'I'm sorry. I shouldn't --'

'It's all right,' Rob told him cheerfully. 'We're used to not hearing things.'

* * *

Since the carriage which had brought Julian's family was blocking the way, it was easy for Adrian and Caroline to get a head start. Mrs Hayward, meanwhile, managed to leave Cassie with no alternative but to invite her to join Adeline, Madeleine and herself for the ride back to Sarre Park. As soon as she saw this, Sylvia allowed herself to gradually fall a little way behind Lavinia and the Langham party ... and a few minutes later, Bertrand arrived at her side, saying with sly humour, 'Should my ears have been burning earlier?'

'You mean they weren't?' Accepting his arm, she slanted a bitter smile at him. 'Once Mama gets an idea in her head, there's no shifting it. I'd apologise for her, except that --'

'Stop. If an apology is due --'

'It isn't. Neither of us did anything wrong, for heaven's sake! So why she jumped to the conclusion that you might ... that *we* might ...' She stopped, not at all sure how to phrase it. 'It's completely ridiculous.'

It was a long time before Bertrand replied. But eventually he said, 'Is it?'

Her breath hitched. 'Is w-what?'

'*Is* it ridiculous?' Her eyes flew to meet his, causing him to say ruefully, 'Forgive me. That was unfair. What I *should* have said is that the possibility of some … attraction … between us is not ridiculous to *me*. But I realise it may be so to you.'

This time the air evaporated from her lungs, making it impossible for her to do more than simply stare at him. But finally she managed to say shyly, 'No. It isn't. Not at all.'

'No?'

'No. I only meant that *Mama* is being ridiculous. And I didn't want you to think that I … that *I* was expecting --' She stopped, clearly impatient with herself. 'Anything. I wasn't expecting *anything*. But I can't pretend I didn't … hope.'

Unprepared for the rush of pleasure her words created and struggling to locate his brain, Bertrand suspected that he was probably grinning like an idiot. However, since she was smiling back at him with something he couldn't quite identify but which made him feel ten feet tall, he murmured, '*Moi aussi*, Sylvie. I also hoped.'

Impossible as it had seemed, her smile grew wider, warmer and sweeter. Typically, however, she said, 'I'm glad – truly I am. But I wish we had more time.'

'What do you mean?'

'Lavinia is missing shopping with her friends and Mama wants to get me as far from you as possible so they're talking about going home the day after tomorrow. And I doubt they'll get any argument from Caroline.'

'What about you? Do *you* want to go?'

'Not in the least. But I won't be given a choice.'

'Perhaps,' said Bertrand slowly, 'I can change that. Will you leave it with me?'

'Yes – of course. But what are you going to do?'

He laughed. 'Right now? Catch up with everyone else before they notice our absence. But later, when I've had a chance to see what I can do, perhaps we can find a few moments of privacy? Only to talk,' he added quickly. 'Nothing else.'

'Nothing at all?'

'No. I promise.'

'Oh.' Sylvia tilted her head and peeped naughtily at him through her lashes. 'That's disappointing.'

CHAPTER TEN

Back at Sarre Park and still stripping off her gloves, Caroline told Croft to be ready to serve wine immediately and, turning to Mrs Holt, added briskly, 'The Dowager Countess will be joining us briefly – she's probably hard on our heels right now. Attend to her yourself, Betsy, so she doesn't terrify one of the maids. I shall be down when I've tidied my hair.'

The housekeeper nodded and muttered something that sounded suspiciously like, 'More ill luck,' under her breath. Adrian, meanwhile, raised satiric brows at his wife and murmured, 'You're leaving me to welcome her? Thank you.'

'Don't mention it. And you won't be alone with her for long. Adeline, Madeleine and Cassie won't be far behind.'

'All of whom will *also* wish to see to their hair or even change their gowns?'

'Oh.' Caroline looked down at her damp hem. 'What a good thing you mentioned that. I'd better hurry.' And she sped off, leaving him glowering at her back.

Good manners giving him no choice but to await his mother's arrival, Adrian dived into the library for a calming nip of brandy and managed to get back to the hall just as her carriage drew up. Mentally cursing and summoning something he hoped might pass for a smile, he went out to the top of the steps to meet her and drawled, 'Welcome to Sarre Park, Madam. It's been a while, hasn't it? You will notice some changes.'

'I notice you appear to have repaired the north wing,' she said sourly. 'One can only hope that the interior décor shows a modicum of taste.'

'But you, of course, doubt that it will. However ... please come inside and judge for yourself. Mrs Holt will look after you and conduct you to the drawing room when you are ready.' And having got her through the door, he strolled away.

The Dowager frowned balefully at Betsy.

'*Mrs* Holt? I do not recall you having ever been married. I *do* recall you having worked in the kitchens – though how that qualifies you for the position of housekeeper is a mystery.'

'Yes, my lady. I daresay it must be,' replied Betsy. 'Allow me to take your hat.'

Wheels on the gravel outside heralded a second carriage.

Ignoring Betsy, the Dowager snapped, 'Who is this arriving?'

'That will be the duchess, Lady Nicholas and Mistress Audley. Does your ladyship wish your hair attended to? If so, I'll summon a maid for you.'

'That will not be necessary. You may take me to my son – since I assume I will not find him in the south parlour.'

'No, my lady. The countess prefers to use the drawing room in the north wing these days. This way, if you please.'

Almost sure she could hear the sound of grinding teeth, Betsy had to hide a smile.

Adrian watched his mother halt a few steps into the room and subject it to a gimlet stare. He knew how badly she wanted to find fault. He also knew that she would struggle to do it, Caroline having chosen a welcoming but elegant combination of rich blues, teamed with buttermilk and good pieces of furniture purloined from other parts of the house so the effect was not overly new.

Eventually, the Dowager remarked, 'That silk rug belongs in the yellow room.'

'It did. Now it belongs here.' Adrian gestured to a sofa near the fire. 'Please ... sit. May I offer you some wine?'

This won him an absent nod, her gaze still busy inspecting the room.

Sighing, he placed a glass on the table at her side, wondering how long it would be before Rockliffe and the others arrived back ... and what on earth he could find to talk about in the interim.

Mercifully, before the conversation could founder completely, Cassie walked in with Madeleine. Both of them curtsied politely to his mother and waited for him to introduce them In typical fashion, the Dowager surveyed Cassie from beneath raised brows and said, 'Audley? Am I to assume that your husband is the wild young man whose various exploits used to fill the scandal sheets?'

'Yes, ma'am.' A martial glint appeared in Cassie's eyes. 'But as your ladyship says, it has been some time since they last did so.'

'Hmm.' The icy stare encompassed Madeleine. 'And you, I believe, are married to Rockliffe's brother. Have I that correctly?'

'Perfectly, ma'am.'

'You are French?' And when Madeleine nodded, 'Of what family?'

'None with whom I imagine your ladyship might be acquainted.' The cool, green eyes turned to Adrian. 'Adeline is bringing the older children down for a short time and --'

'*Children*?' echoed the Dowager, sounding appalled. 'In the *drawing* room? At *this* time of day? Preposterous!'

'Oh – for God's sake!' snapped Adrian. 'It's Christmas. We're hardly going to confine them to the nursery except for the statutory half-hour before tea.'

'Why not? It is perfectly adequate.'

'It's certainly all Ben and I ever saw of you,' he retorted. 'And since you've yet to clap eyes on your grandson, I'd have thought you might have *some* interest in seeing him – if only because he will be the next earl.'

There was a brief, deathly silence. Then, looking at Adrian, Cassie said incredulously, 'She lives in the *Dower House* and she's never seen Benedict?' And when Adrian nodded, she turned back to his mother and added, 'You may not care much for Caroline or even your son – but is it beyond you even to be a grandmother?'

'How dare you!' The Dowager surged to her feet. 'It is not for you to judge either me or my relationship with my son and the ill-bred female he has married – neither of which are any of your business. You take too much upon yourself and I will hear your apology.'

Adrian's growl of, 'That's *enough*!' clashed with Sebastian's, '*What* apology?' and caused everyone to swivel towards the doorway where Rockliffe, together with Nicholas, Julian and Tom, stood two steps behind Mr Audley. And a little way behind *them* were gathering Adeline with Vanessa on one hand and John on the other ... and Caroline carrying Benedict.

Cassie merely made a vague gesture with one hand and shook her head, thus allowing Adrian to say, 'I asked you to show my wife some respect, Madam. Since you refuse to do so and cannot even --'

'I give respect where it is due – namely to those with birth and breeding.'

'--- show a modicum of interest in our son,' he continued as if she had not spoken, 'I suggest you take your leave.'

'I shall leave,' announced the Dowager, resuming her seat, 'when I am ready. First, now some of your guests appear to have re-joined us, you may present them to me.'

Adrian's mouth curled unpleasantly. Turning his head, he said, 'I think she means you, Rock ... and possibly Adeline and Julian, as well. Do any of you wish to meet my mother?'

There was another long, airless silence before the duke said languidly, 'Forgive me, Adrian. I believe I must reserve that … pleasure … for another occasion.'

Caroline's jaw dropped, Cassie gasped and Sebastian gave a tiny snort of laughter.

'Julian?' asked Adrian. 'Nicholas? Anyone?' And when no one spoke, 'It seems you'll have to hold them excused, ma'am. Some other time, perhaps?'

Eyes snapping with temper and rare colour staining her cheekbones, the Dowager rose majestically to her feet. 'That is unlikely. Clearly your wife's ill-manners are contagious. And that being so, I shall not expose myself to further insult. I will bid you all good day.'

'And we bid you the same,' he replied, with the merest hint of a bow. 'Tom – be a good fellow and ask Croft to have the Dowager Countess's carriage brought round, will you? Her ladyship won't wish to be kept waiting.'

Head held high, the Dowager swept from the room without even glancing at her grandson. As soon as she was out of earshot, Sebastian said wickedly, 'Brrr! There's a real chill in the air. Has the fire gone out?'

'No,' muttered Caroline, not quite beneath her breath as she ushered everyone into the drawing-room and signalled to the footman to serve wine. 'It's just the Ice Queen effect.'

He grinned at her. 'I know it well. You've never met my sister Blanche, have you?' And when she shook her head, 'We ought to introduce her to the Dowager. They'd either become bosom bows or one of them would murder the other. Hard to say which.'

Sighing, Adrian said, 'My apologies to you all. And my thanks.

'Your thanks for what?' asked Cassie. 'The fact that we answered the countess's rudeness with some of our own? Speaking for myself, I feel rather awful for *not* feeling awful – if you know what I mean.'

'Blame it on Rock,' advised Nicholas. 'He started it. I've never met anyone else who can manage to make a direct snub sound perfectly polite.'

'You've been delivering one of your famous snubs, Rock?' enquired Amberley, sauntering in trailed by Rob and Ellie. 'Perhaps to the lady who almost flattened Ellie on her way through the door just now?'

'The very one,' murmured Rockliffe.

'Oh God.' Adrian groaned. 'Did she hurt you, Ellie?'

'No. I don't think she *meant* to push me. She was just in a hurry.' She thought for a moment and then added, 'But I'm quite glad she's gone.'

'We all are,' Cassie told her. 'Now ... where are all the other ladies?'

'Changing their gowns because their hems were soggy. All except Miss Sylvia, that is. She was walking with Mr Bertrand and they got left behind the rest of us.' Ellie looked longingly at the trays of tiny fruit tartlets the footman had just brought in. 'Please may I have one of those?'

'Have two, darling,' laughed Sebastian. 'You too, Rob – before Mama-Belle comes down and tells you not to spoil your appetite. After all, we've been to church and had our fresh air and exercise for the day ... so now we're allowed to have fun. What do you say?'

The enthusiastic chorus of '*Yes!*' that answered him did not come solely from the children.

* * *

After everyone had taken some refreshment and small gifts had been exchanged, Bertrand took charge of the afternoon's entertainment. A succession of increasingly noisy parlour games drew forth laughter and good-humoured arguments; hilarious forfeits were dreamed up and paid with even more hilarious results; kisses were stolen under the mistletoe. And later, when the youngest children had been returned, exhausted, to the nursery, the adults sat down at a table virtually groaning under the weight of the Christmas feast. Succulent goose, beef and hams jostled with an array of vegetables and numerous sauces; salmon nudged trout and turbot; an enormous Chantilly cream loomed over a selection of tarts and syllabubs. And throughout all of it, Adrian ensured the footmen kept everyone's glasses filled with a succession of excellent wines.

And later still, when even Tom and Rob had gone upstairs yawning, there were cards accompanied by witty (and sometimes risqué) conversation. There was also music ... because everyone insisted that the Virtuoso Earl couldn't be expected to resist the lure of the keyboard for an entire day. So Julian played ... sometimes Mozart or Haydn and sometimes popular songs which everyone could join in ... and the evening passed in a companionable haze of wine and lazy relaxation.

* * *

Bertrand waited until everyone's attention was centred on Julian before catching Sylvia's eye and slipping unobtrusively from the room. Despite the excitement fizzing through her veins, Sylvia made herself wait for four whole minutes before, murmuring an excuse about looking for her fan (which she'd had the sense to 'misplace' earlier) and slipping out after him. A swift glance about the hall revealed it empty of servants and Bertrand lurking in the doorway of a room which she had never entered but knew to be Adrian's study. Sylvia picked up her skirts, ran to him in a rustle of sea-green silk ... and immediately found herself whisked inside and into his arms.

Bertrand wasn't sure how that had happened. He certainly hadn't intended it to. But when he saw her smile ... when he watched her skimming towards him ... all good sense and sterling intentions fled before what was suddenly inevitable. And then her arms were about his neck and her mouth was drugging him with heat and sweetness and he couldn't have let go of her if his life had depended on it.

Equally heedless, Sylvia's only (and very fleeting) thought was to wonder how, in the space of such a short time, she had come to feel this way about Bertrand Didier; and to marvel at the sheer *rightness* of it ... as if she had finally come home. So she kissed him back, pressing her body close against his, sliding her fingers into his hair and letting herself simply drown in him.

Bertrand retained just enough sense not to go *beyond* kissing, much though he'd have liked to. Knowing that they would not be disturbed here added another layer of temptation to something which was already nigh on irresistible. But it wouldn't do for Sylvie to return to the drawing-room looking disarranged. Not until he knew his own mind and she hers. And for that, they needed to talk.

Reluctantly releasing her mouth but not quite ready to relinquish the rest of her, he murmured wryly, 'Well ... my word wasn't worth much, was it?'

Sylvia's eyes fluttered slowly open and she said hazily, 'What?'

He smiled, unable to help basking in her response.

'I promised conversation and nothing more.'

'Oh. So you did.' She smiled back at him and, seeming to realise that her arms were still around his neck, let her hands slide to his shoulders. 'It was a silly promise.'

'It was?'

'Yes. But very well-meant and honourable.'

'Good intentions don't count. According to Saint Bernard of Clairvaux, the road to hell is paved with them.' Stepping back to take her hands in his, Bertrand grinned suddenly. 'I've spoken to Adrian. If you wish to extend your visit after your mother and sister go home, you are invited to do so.'

'Really?' Her eyes lit up and then clouded. 'Mama won't let me.'

'Caroline says she can persuade her. So ... will you stay?'

'I – yes. Oh yes!' Sylvia laughed up at him. 'Thank you!'

'You can thank me by saving at least two dances for me tomorrow evening.'

'I'd give you all of them,' she said, reaching up to kiss his cheek, 'except Mama would probably have an apoplexy.'

Which might be no bad thing if it stops the wretched woman talking, thought Bertrand. But had the sense not to say it.

* * *

At around the time Bertrand and Sylvia were slipping discreetly out of Adrian's study, another clandestine meeting was taking place in the library – although, to be fair, this one had not been planned. In Sylvia's absence, Lily and Adeline had been discussing the girl's determination to improve her education by reading.

'Which is very laudable, of course,' remarked Lily. 'But she's missing the pleasures of a good novel. She hasn't read anything at all by Samuel Richardson or Mr Fielding – which seems a shame.'

'Recommend something, then,' suggested Adeline. 'The new one people are saying was written by a female … *Evelina*, is it?'

'*The Castle of Otranto*,' volunteered Cassie. And with a gurgle of laughter, 'Do you remember the house on Mount Street, Sebastian?'

He glanced up from his cards, shuddering slightly. 'I try not to.'

'It was horrid. Dark and gloomy, full of cobwebs and decorated with dead animals,' she said cheerfully. 'But being scared is fun when it's between the pages of a book.'

'That's true … and I'm sure there's a copy of *Otranto* in the library.' Lily rose from her chair. 'I'll fetch it and talk Sylvia into trying it.'

Mr Maitland watched her leave the room and thought, *Ten minutes left of Christmas Day and probably nobody in the library but her. If I'm going to chance my arm, I reckon now'd be a good time for it. And if somebody wants to make something of me following her, let 'em. No skin off my nose what anybody else thinks, is it?*

Tossing aside the periodical he'd been glancing through, he stood up and strode purposefully from the room.

He found Lily, hands on hips, scowling at a bookshelf. 'What's the trouble, lass?'

The scowl vanished and she turned to him, laughing. '*Lass*? Hubert, I haven't been a lass for thirty years.'

'Maybe not. But you looked like one when you was playing charades and trying to do Hannibal's elephants.'

She groaned. 'Don't! Why did *I* have to be the one to draw Sebastian's ticket? Everyone else's suggestions were perfectly sane.

But an elephant? Who can pantomime an elephant without looking ridiculous?'

Hubert thought she'd looked adorable; flushed, breathless and with her hair coming adrift from its pins. It had been the moment he'd finally known what he was going to do. He said, 'I don't suppose many have had occasion to try. And you didn't look ridiculous, Lily. You looked happy ... and so pretty a man'd have to be blind not to notice.'

'Oh.' Her heart gave a little lurch and she eyed him uncertainly. 'That is a – a lovely thing to say. But really you sh-shouldn't --'

He narrowed the space between them so that he could take her hands.

'Hear me out before you tell me what I shouldn't say. And make allowances for me being a plain man with no talent for fancy words.' He paused, holding her gaze with his. 'I've enjoyed your company these last days more than I've enjoyed anything in a very long time, Lily Brassington – and I'll be sorrier than I can say when they come to an end. So here's the thing. I never expected I'd want to wed again ... but then again, I never expected to meet a warm, lovely woman like you. Now I have, I don't want to let you get away. So do you think there's any chance you might make me the happiest old fellow in Yorkshire?'

At some point while he'd been speaking, the hall clock had begun chiming midnight and hadn't yet finished. For what seemed the longest minute of his life, Lily simply stared at him out of eyes luminous with shock turning slowly to something he couldn't interpret. Finally she said softly, 'Are you ... are you quite *sure*, Hubert?'

'Aye, love. Do you think I'd have asked if I wasn't?'

'No. No, of course you wouldn't. It was a silly question. It – it's just that you have taken me so completely by surprise that my wits are a bit scrambled.'

He smiled and squeezed her fingers. 'I understand that well enough. Truth to tell, I'm a bit surprised myself.'

'Yes. I imagine you must be.'

'And I know it'd be a bigger step for you than for me what with all you'd be giving up – so you'll need time to consider. All I'm asking now is if you think it *worth* considering.'

Lily took a deep breath and smiled shyly back at him. 'It would be ... if I needed to. But I don't.'

'Ah.' He tried not to let the disappointment show. 'Well, you're probably right. And I hope you didn't mind me asking.'

'Mind you *asking*? Oh, you foolish man! As if I could. And I don't want to *consider* your offer because I already know my answer.'

'You do?'

She nodded, beaming at him. 'I do … and it's yes. *Yes*, Hubert Maitland, I'll marry you – and be proud to be your wife. As for what you think I'd be giving up … I can't think of a single thing that I'd miss or that matters to me in the slightest.'

Just for a moment, with exultation flooding through him like a tide, Hubert didn't know what to do. And then he did. He put his arms around her and kissed her. And Lily, his lovely, sweet Lily, threw her arms about his neck and kissed him back.

CHAPTER ELEVEN

They returned to the drawing-room separately and, belatedly remembering about *The Castle of Otranto*, Lily said she had hunted high and low but been unable to find it. Then, on the following morning directly after breakfast and before the inevitable turmoil of preparation for that evening's St Stephen's Ball began, she and Hubert shared their happy news with Adrian and Caroline.

'*Betrothed*?' echoed Caroline. 'You – the two of you are getting *married*?'

'Aye, lass. That's where a betrothal usually leads, isn't it? And I don't reckon it comes as *that* big a shock.'

'No. No – and it's wonderful!' Caroline drew Lily into a fierce hug. 'I'm so happy for you – for *both* of you.'

'As am I.' Adrian grasped Hubert's hand. 'Heartfelt congratulations, sir. I have no doubt that you'll be very happy.'

Whatever reply Hubert might have made was lost when he found his arms full of his grand-daughter. This gave Adrian the opportunity to kiss Lily's hand, saying, 'I'm delighted for you ... and deeply impressed that you managed not to tell everyone last night. At least – I assume that *is* when he proposed?'

She nodded, seemingly unable to stop smiling. 'On the stroke of midnight.'

'Very romantic. And if the two of you can continue to keep the secret until this evening, perhaps you'd allow me to announce it at the ball?'

'Oh yes!' enthused Caroline. 'That would be marvellous – a real celebration.'

Tucking Lily's hand in his arm, Hubert said, 'I reckon we might manage to keep the cat in the bag till then ... if that's all right with you, love?'

'Yes. It's more than all right.' She beamed at him. 'It would be perfect.'

* * *

Ten minutes later when Adrian was about to consult with his butler over the evening's wines, he was waylaid by his mother-in-law who said briskly, 'The girls and me haven't the right clothes with us for tonight so we'll need to go back and fetch 'em.'

'That is not a problem. Ask Bertrand to have a carriage brought round.'

'After the trouble he's caused, I'm having nowt to do with that young rascal.'

Oh don't be so bloody ridiculous, thought Adrian. But said curtly, 'Then speak to Croft.' And when she showed no sign of moving away, 'Was there anything else?'

'Yes. I think it'll be best all round if we was to go back to Twickenham tomorrow. But we'll need a carriage for *that* an' all.'

'Of course. My travelling chaise will be at your disposal.' Trying not to look too cheerful and recalling his promise to Bertrand, he said, 'May I ask what caused this sudden decision?'

'Lavvy and me are ready to go home anyway ... and there'll be a dance at the White Lion for Twelfth Night with plenty of single gentlemen in attendance.' She paused, before adding, 'And I want Syl away from here before any more harm's done.'

'Sylvia? Ah. Hasn't Caroline told you?'

'Told me what?'

'That she has invited Sylvia to stay with us a little longer and --'

'*What*? Nobody's said a word about that to me!'

'Yet,' said Adrian calmly. 'Clearly Caroline hasn't had the opportunity to speak to you *yet*. The notion of Sylvia remaining to keep her company after the rest of the guests have left us only occurred to her last night. I agreed that it was a good idea.'

'Well, it's not. And it isn't happening.'

'Surely the choice must be Sylvia's?' he suggested. And before she could answer, 'However, I suggest you take this up with Caroline – though not this morning because she is extremely busy. As am I, in fact. So if you'll excuse me?' And he walked away, grateful to escape but uneasily aware that he'd left Caroline in the eye of the coming storm.

The storm broke over Sylvia the moment the carriage door closed behind them.

'What's this nonsense about you not coming home with us?' demanded Mrs Hayward irately. 'And why wasn't I told about it?'

'Since you're asking, obviously you *must* have been,' shrugged Sylvia. 'But if you mean why didn't *I* tell you, this is the first time I've had the chance – because I wasn't about to start an argument over the breakfast table.'

'What's going on?' asked Lavinia. 'Are you really staying behind?'

'No, she isn't,' snapped Mrs Hayward.

'Yes,' said Sylvia composedly, 'I am. Caroline invited me and I accepted. It will only be for a couple of weeks and --'

'Over my dead body. You think I'll leave you here to play ducks and drakes with your reputation? I won't. And don't try telling me this was Caro's idea. It wasn't. That sly French fellow's talked her into it, hasn't he? *Hasn't* he?'

'Not that I'm aware of,' came the not entirely untruthful reply. 'Why don't you ask him?'

'And have him lie to my face? I'll not waste my breath. We're going to get what we need for tonight and tomorrow and pack everything else ready to be loaded on the carriage in the morning. *You*, my girl, will be coming home to Twickenham with Lavvy and me – and that's my last word.'

'Good,' said Sylvia. 'Because talking until you go blue won't make a jot of difference. And unless you want to make a spectacle of yourself trying to drag me away, there isn't a lot you can do about it.'

'Isn't there? I'll wager Caro will change her tune fast enough when she knows I've said no,' announced Mrs Hayward triumphantly. 'She's always been a dutiful girl – and she won't gainsay her own mother.'

Lavinia laughed. 'I wouldn't be too sure about that, Mam. Have you forgotten the way she laid down the law when we first got here?'

'That was different.'

'Not as I can see. Caro's a countess now. And I reckon she'll do as she likes.'

* * *

Preparations for the ball continued throughout the day. It would be a relatively small affair by London standards; but in addition to their houseguests, Lord and Lady Sarre had invited the vicar, the doctor and all five families living within relatively easy distance – most of whom had sons and daughters already out in society and thus bringing the total guest list to forty-two.

'Which is quite sufficient,' observed Adrian to Caroline, 'given that the ballroom isn't especially large. But you can congratulate yourself on holding a ball at all, my love. It will be the first in this house during my lifetime.'

Croft supervised the removal of chairs to the ballroom and the setting up of an area for the small orchestra engaged for the evening. Madeleine instructed footmen in the placement of big tubs of hot-house flowers and more festive greenery. Mrs Holt and Cook had the kitchen under full production for a light, mid-afternoon repast for the houseguests and the lavish buffet supper to be served later in the evening. Bertrand turned the winter parlour into a card room. And Caroline ran to and fro, conferring and double-checking that nothing had been forgotten and all was in perfect order.

Then, just when it seemed that everything that could be done, *had* been done and Caroline thought she could put her feet up for half an hour, Sylvia arrived at her bedchamber door in a state of agitation.

She said rapidly, 'I wasn't able to speak with you this morning but Bertrand says you and his lordship don't mind if I stay here for a little while after Mama and Lavinia leave. That's right, isn't it?'

Conversation with Adrian on this point having been minimal, Caroline said, 'Yes. Of course, if that's what you want.'

'It is. Thank you. And – and you won't change your mind, will you?'

'No.' Caroline's instincts suddenly advised caution. 'Why would you think I might?'

'Because Mama's going to try and make you. She's probably looking for you right now.'

'Oh God. As if I don't have enough to do today.'

'I know – and I'm sorry.'

'So am I. However ... I suppose this is because of Bertrand?'

'Yes.'

Sighing inwardly, Caroline waved her sister into a chair and said, 'Do you want to tell me about it? You don't have to if you'd prefer not ... but it might help.'

Sylvia hesitated, twisting her hands together and then, as if the words were bursting from her, 'I think ... I think I might be in love with him, Caro. And I think ... I *hope* ... he might feel the same, though he hasn't said so or – or anything definite at *all* as yet. But it's only been a few days and what with the snow and wishes and kissing boughs ...' She hesitated and then added, 'I think what's between me and Bertrand is real but it's happened so quick it's taken us both by surprise. We need a bit of time. But if I go home tomorrow that won't happen and – and I could lose him. Do you understand?'

'Yes. And you're being very sensible. It's a pity Mama can't see that.'

'All *she* can see is that Bertrand isn't rich and titled,' came the bitter reply. 'But I don't care about that. When I'm with him everything inside me seems to - to *hum* – and yet it just feels *right*. Does that sound silly?'

'No. It sounds serious.'

'So you won't give in to Mama?'

'No. I won't. And if she starts haranguing me about this today I'm likely to tip a bowl of blancmange over her head.'

Sylvia laughed, gave her sister a hug and departed with a spring in her step. As soon as she had gone, Caroline summoned her maid and said grimly, 'I am going to retire to my bedchamber, Polly. *You* are going to guard the door.'

'Yes, my lady. Against everyone?'

'Everyone except his lordship and *particularly* against my mother. Tell her I'm asleep or in the bath or practising black magic. Tell her anything you like – but do *not* let her in.'

* * *

Baulked in her attempt to gain access to Caroline, Mrs Hayward tracked down Adrian instead and, butting into his conversation with Mr Audley, said baldly, 'I've told Syl she's to come home with Lavvy and me. I'll expect Caro to cancel this invitation of hers before the evening's out.'

Sebastian blinked but wisely kept his mouth shut.

Adrian said coolly, 'I think that unlikely. And as I remarked earlier, I believe that Sylvia is entitled to have some say in the matter.'

'She's got *no* say in it – and neither have you! Syl's not of age and I'm her *mother* – so you and Caro have got no business encouraging her to defy me.'

'Then perhaps you should consider adopting a more reasonable attitude.'

Mrs Hayward virtually ground her teeth. 'I'm not leaving her here to throw herself away on that dratted Frenchie. She's coming home tomorrow if I have to drag her into the carriage myself.'

'Good luck with that,' murmured Sebastian.

'Indeed,' nodded Adrian. And to his enraged mother-in-law, 'Don't expect help. You won't get it.'

'The only help *I* need is Caro doing what she's told – but that uppity maid of hers won't let me in the room to talk to her.'

'That is probably for the best. Addressing Caroline in the way you are addressing me is unlikely to advance your cause. However, I will pass on your point of view to her in due course. And now, perhaps you might leave Mr Audley and me to finish our conversation?' And he turned his back on her.

Mrs Hayward's hands clenched. She opened her mouth on a hasty retort but closed it again when Sebastian said blandly, 'Oh don't mind me, Adrian. Other people's squabbling relatives are always *so* much more entertaining than one's own, don't you find?' Upon which, she flounced out, letting the door slam behind her.

Adrian looked at Mr Audley and said, 'Do you have to be so bloody annoying?'

'Be grateful. I got rid of her, didn't I?'

* * *

Everyone gathered in the drawing-room a half hour before the neighbouring guests were expected to begin arriving. The ladies were resplendent in plain or patterned silks of every possible hue ... the gentlemen, in rich shades of exquisitely tailored velvet and brocade. Jewels flashed in the candlelight and fans fluttered. Dance cards were asked for, produced and signed. Sylvia, clad in a new gown of ice-blue watered taffeta, was awed to find herself engaged to dance with Mr Audley, Lord Chalfont and the Marquis of Amberley. And a few moments later while her mother was being held in conversation with Lady Brassington, Bertrand was at her side murmuring, 'You look beautiful, Sylvie. Have you a dance left for me?'

'Two. The ones either side of supper – and I've already written your name beside them,' she said, before adding rapidly, 'Mama's insisting I go home tomorrow but Caroline says I need not.'

'I know. And fortunately, your mama has thoroughly annoyed Adrian.'

'How is that fortunate?'

He smiled. 'Because if she wants his help, that isn't the way to get it. Now ... I should go before she sees us together and forbids you to dance with me. But I will find you later and meanwhile enjoy yourself ... though perhaps not *too* much.'

On the other side of the room, Mr Maitland contemplated his newly-betrothed, positively glowing in amber satin, and wondered at his good fortune. He said, 'Lily, love ... you look a picture. The prettiest woman in the room and no mistake.'

She blushed a little and rapped his wrist with her fan. 'You are flattering me. But I don't mind a bit – so please go on.'

'It's not flattery. To my mind, you *are* the prettiest woman here. If you weren't, I wouldn't be about to do summat I haven't done in twenty years or more.'

'Which is what?' she asked.

'Dance,' he replied heroically.

* * *

An hour later, the ball was in full swing. Houseguests and neighbours mingled happily; having opened the ball with Adeline while

Caroline danced with Rockliffe, Adrian did his duty by all the other ladies; and, between dances with the doctor and the vicar, Caroline spent time chatting with the older ladies who chose to watch rather than participate. Even Mrs Hayward found nothing to complain about to begin with. Lavinia had been led out by Lord Amberley and had subsequently been virtually fought over by three young gentlemen, one of whose father was a baron. And Sylvia had progressed from Mr Audley to the Virtuoso Earl and was so far showing no sign of searching the room for Monsieur Didier.

Despite his misgivings, Mr Maitland managed to lead Lady Brassington through a gavotte – during which Cassie and Arabella noticed with interest that the pair didn't seem to be able to take their eyes off each other. Nearly everyone quit the floor to watch and (in the case of the ladies) sigh as Lord Amberley guided his lovely marchioness through a minuet. And as the supper dance approached, Bertrand finally abandoned his self-appointed task of keeping a watchful eye on how much the youngest gentlemen were drinking and went to claim Sylvia for the quadrille.

He said, 'Since you've danced every dance, I won't ask if you are enjoying yourself.'

'I enjoyed myself because I had *this* to look forward to,' she retorted. 'And how do *you* know how much I've danced? You've spent much of the evening in the card room.'

He shrugged. 'Shall I name every partner you've had?'

'Can you?'

'Yes.' He leaned a little closer and murmured, 'Don't tell anyone … but I can see through walls.'

Sylvia gave a choke of laughter. 'Really?'

'Really.'

'Well, that is *definitely* something you'd want to keep quiet about.'

'Yes. Only imagine what might happen to me if word got out.' The music began and, offering his hand, he led her to join an as yet incomplete set. 'And if anyone was foolish enough to believe it.'

She laughed again and shook her head at him. 'Some people will believe anything. You know that.'

The quadrille was half over before Mrs Hayward looked up from a conversation with the vicar's wife and saw with whom Sylvia was dancing. Her fingers clenched around her fan and she scowled, causing the vicar's wife to say, 'Are you quite well, ma'am? You are very flushed. Perhaps a glass of ratafia?'

'No. That is – I'm just a bit warm. I believe I'll take a turn in the hall.' And she stalked away without waiting for Mrs Murdoch to reply.

She did not, however, go into the hall. She went only as far as the doorway because she was damned if she was going to let Sylvia slip off somewhere with Bertrand Didier. Consequently, as the quadrille ended, she was so intent on keeping the guilty pair in sight that she didn't immediately notice what was happening at the front of the room. It wasn't until the orchestra played a brief fanfare and everyone fell silent that she realised Adrian was about to address the company.

'Ladies and gentlemen,' he began. 'Supper will be served in the drawing-room across the hall. But before you enjoy some well-earned refreshment, my wife and I have the very great pleasure of sharing some happy news. We are delighted to announce the betrothal of Caroline's grandfather, Mr Hubert Maitland and our dear friend, Lily, Lady Brassington. Please join us in wishing them well.'

Mrs Hayward scarcely heard the good-natured applause through the buzzing in her ears. She did, however, hear Sebastian Audley shouting, 'Bravo, Mr Maitland! Well done indeed, sir!'

Lavinia emerged at her side and said smugly, 'Told you, Mam.'

'Silly old fool,' sniffed her mother. 'Doesn't he know she's only after his money?'

'Not according to what she's been saying to Syl, she isn't.'

'Forget what she's *said*. She's hardly going to admit it, is she? And why else would she have him?'

'Well, I think it's sweet,' insisted Lavinia. And changing to an even trickier subject, 'What are you going to do about Syl?'

'I'll decide that when I've spoken to Caro – if I ever do.'

'Avoiding you, is she?' And without waiting for an answer, 'Mr Eversley's coming over. He's taking me in to supper. His father's a baron, you know.'

Mrs Hayward stayed where she was as guests filed past her laughing and talking. She lost sight of Sylvia for a few moments before spotting her arm in arm with Cassie Audley. Of Bertrand, there was no sign at all ... but that hardly mattered so long as he wasn't with Sylvia. Then she saw Caroline heading in her direction whilst chatting animatedly with Lady B. Mrs Hayward waited and as soon as she had the chance, reached out to grasp her daughter's wrist, saying baldly, 'I want to talk to you.'

Caroline sighed and tried, without success, to pull her hand free. 'I am not going to argue with you now, Mama.'

'Good. Because I'm taking Syl home tomorrow – and you'll stop encouraging her to disobey me.'

'Didn't you hear what I said? We are not discussing this now.'

'And I say we *will*!'

From behind them Adrian's voice suddenly said, 'Mrs Hayward – release Caroline's wrist. Now.'

She flushed and reluctantly loosed her grip. 'I only wanted to --'

'I believe we are all aware what you wanted but this is neither the time nor the place. I wish to hear no more of it this evening. So perhaps you might be good enough to stop obstructing the doorway and allow our other guests to go in to supper?'

Just for a second, she hesitated. Then she spun on her heel and walked away.

Accepting Adrian's arm, Caroline whispered, 'What are we going to do with her?'

'Not,' he replied grimly, 'what I would like. Unfortunately.'

Inside the supper room Hubert and Lily were deluged with congratulations and sincere good wishes. Then everyone found seats and filled plates while footmen circulated with trays of chilled wine and champagne. Mrs Hayward descended on Lavinia and Mr Eversley and stared balefully at the large table where Sylvia sat laughing with Cassie and Madeleine. On the opposite side of it, Bertrand seemed to be joking with Sebastian and Lord Nicholas ... and the three of them were presently joined by Adrian.

Later, when everyone had eaten and drunk their fill and were beginning to head back to the ballroom, Adrian pulled up a chair beside Bertrand and said bluntly, 'If you were thinking of dancing with Sylvia again – don't. In fact, stay away from her for the rest of the evening. If you do that there's a small chance her damned mother may stop trying to force a quarrel on Caroline – and thus prevent me resorting to violence.'

Bertrand nodded. 'I was promised to Sylvie for the next dance.'

'I'll take your place and explain to her. All we have to do is get through the next few hours. I'll send the carriage to collect the rest of their luggage from Devereux House first thing in the morning. Once it's here, Croft will have Sylvia's trunk unloaded and stowed out of sight. Then you and she will merely have to lie low until Mrs Hayward accepts defeat and leaves. How hard can it be?'

'I don't know.' Bertrand rose, shrugging. 'But I have a nasty feeling that we'll find out.'

CHAPTER TWELVE

After yet another argument with Sylvia and the situation still not resolved to her satisfaction, Mrs Hayward retired in a very bad temper and a mood of implacable determination. Reading her mother's expression without difficulty and dreading the inevitable hour-long tirade in their bedchamber, Lavinia was surprised when it did not come. Instead, her mother readied herself for bed without a single word, then blew out the candle and lay staring up into the dark. Somewhat unnerved by this, Lavinia briefly considered inviting conversation ... then decided that silence was infinitely preferable.

It was nearly two hours later that Mrs Hayward suddenly sat up in the grip of a new and very simple idea. She turned it over and over in her mind for a time, planning how to put it in motion. Then, certain that it was infallible, she lay down and slept.

On the following morning, Sylvia entered the breakfast parlour with Lily expecting to find her mother lying in wait to ambush her and instead found the room occupied by only the Audleys, Lord and Lady Nicholas, Mr Maitland and Lavinia. Taking a seat next to her sister, she said hollowly, 'Where is she?'

'I don't know. By the time I woke up, she was almost dressed and not long after she went off saying she'd see me later.' Lavinia reached for the raspberry preserve. 'Since Caro's not here neither, you can bet Mam's got her cornered.'

'Oh God. I hope not – or his lordship will probably smother her.'

'Or send you home with us just to shut her up?'

'Yes. Or that.'

Lavinia looked at her with interest and whispered, 'Do you *really* like Mr Didier?'

'Yes. I really do. And that's the only question I'm answering.'

The door opened upon Rockliffe and Amberley, swiftly followed by Caroline. Just as Sylvia had done, she glanced around the table and then, visibly relaxing, said, 'Good morning, everyone. After such a late night and having left Adeline, Rosalind and Arabella in the nursery, I'd half-expected to be breakfasting alone today.'

'We're not *that* feeble,' retorted Sebastian. 'I'm for a ride this morning – if anyone cares to join me.'

'I'll come,' said Amberley.

'Me too,' nodded Nicholas. 'Rock?'

The duke exhibited signs of mild interest.

'Are you intending to try out the horse you bought in Canterbury?'

'Yes.'

'Then I wouldn't miss it.'

Amberley laughed. 'And the rest of us can listen to the two of you bickering.'

'I,' sighed Rockliffe, 'do not bicker.' And then, as the door opened again to admit Adrian and Bertrand, followed in his usual desultory fashion by Julian, 'Excellent. Some of us are planning to ride this morning. Will any of you be joining us?'

'Not me.' Bertrand wasted no time heading for the food. 'I promised this morning to Tom and Rob.'

'And I need to practise,' said Julian, to the usual chorus of good-natured groans.

'If you delay your departure until after Caroline's mother has made hers,' said Adrian, 'I'll come.'

'We should do that anyway,' observed the duke, taking the seat beside Julian, 'as a matter of common courtesy.'

'Something which has been notable by its absence lately,' murmured Sebastian.

'True as it may be, that remark might have been better left unsaid,' observed Rockliffe gently. 'May we assume that Mrs Hayward *is* leaving today?'

'God willing,' breathed Adrian.

'But Sylvie is not?' asked Bertrand, carrying a laden plate to the table.

'That is the plan.'

And, 'Not if I can help it,' muttered Sylvia. 'I'm so sorry to cause all this trouble.'

'No one blames you,' began Caroline, then stopped as the butler entered the room looking fraught. 'Yes, Croft? What is it?'

Croft looked unhappily at Adrian.

'Excuse me, my lord ... but have the orders you gave me last night been changed?'

Adrian's eyes narrowed and he set down his still empty plate.

'They have not. Why?'

'I had to leave the hall for a few minutes. During my absence, the carriage arrived from Devereux House with the ladies' luggage. Mrs Hayward ordered Robert and Joseph to bring in *all* of it and to have it conveyed upstairs. Then she told Harris to return the carriage to the stables because it would not be needed after all.'

Everyone stopped eating and there was a brief breathless hush into which Sebastian said irreverently, 'Good strategy. I didn't know Mrs Hayward played chess.'

Ignoring him, Adrian's gaze remained focussed on the butler.

'Exactly how was this allowed to happen?'

'It – it was the newspapers, my lord,' replied Croft unhappily. 'They arrived later than usual and I had to take them downstairs to --'

'You left the hall to iron the *newspapers*?' snapped Adrian. And before the unfortunate butler could reply, 'Never mind. Where is Mrs Hayward now?'

'I believe she has had breakfast served to her in the south parlour, my lord.'

'Has she indeed?'

'I don't understand,' said Lavinia in bewilderment. 'Why would Mam do that?'

'Oh I think that is fairly clear,' said Adrian. 'Croft ... ask Mrs Hayward to join us here.'

'No.' Caroline came swiftly to her feet. 'Adrian, no. We shouldn't be inflicting this on everyone else. *I'll* talk to Mama and ask what she thinks she's doing --'

'I know *precisely* what she's doing – and so must nearly everyone in this room. She is holding a metaphorical gun to Sylvia's head and to yours – and she thinks, very stupidly, that I will let her do it. *Croft!* Why are you still here?'

The butler fled; Caroline sank back into her seat and closed her eyes; Sylvia stared miserably across at Bertrand. Nearly everyone else went back to their breakfasts and tried to look uninterested.

It was Rockliffe who eventually broke the silence by saying dispassionately, 'One would like, at this point, to say something encouraging, Adrian. However ... if you hope to *embarrass* the lady into submission, I would have to admit that I consider it unlikely.'

'Not unlikely,' muttered Caroline. 'Impossible.'

'Will somebody please tell me what is going *on*?' demanded Lavinia plaintively.

Catching an expression of *God! Is she really that dense?* on Adrian's face, Cassie stepped swiftly into the breach. She said, 'It seems your Mama has decided that if Sylvia won't leave, none of you will. And having had all your things brought into the house, she believes that Caroline will have no choice but to accept it.'

Adrian gave a hard laugh. 'Over my dead body.'

'Yes. I think we've all gathered that,' agreed Sebastian, composedly cutting up a sausage. 'Just out of interest ... what do *you* think of all this, Mr Maitland?'

Hubert's brows rose. 'What I've always thought. Maria Hayward was behind the door when the brains were dished out. And Adrian's in the right of it, Caroline. If you let good manners force you into a corner, you'll live to regret it. Send her packing. That's my advice.'

It was perhaps inevitable that Mrs Hayward should enter the room in time to hear this. She said belligerently, 'I'll thank you to keep your opinions to yourself, Hubert Maitland.'

'Aye. You'd like that, wouldn't you? Mine and everybody else's.'

Ignoring this, she swept round to locate Adrian, saying, 'Well, I'm here. So say what you've got to say.'

Caroline groaned. 'Don't make this worse than it needs to be, Mama. Some small show of manners wouldn't hurt.'

Mrs Hayward ignored that as well and continued to stare at Adrian over folded arms.

A faint but extremely disquieting smile hovering about his mouth, he said, 'I am told that, contrary to previous intentions, you have had your luggage brought in and sent the carriage away. Perhaps you can explain why.'

'It's simple enough, isn't it? This is what comes of you and Caro going against me and letting Syl stay here when I've said she can't. So if Syl's not coming home, Lavvy and me aren't going neither – and there's an end of it.'

'I see. Anything else?'

'Yes. I'll be keeping a close eye on *him*.' She stabbed a finger in Bertrand's direction. 'So I'll be staying *here* in *this* house – no more fobbing me off with t'other one. I've had enough of that.'

Adrian managed not to remark that he had had enough of quite a number of things – most notably *her*. He said, 'In short, you are inviting yourself for an extended visit.'

'If you want to put it like that.'

'There's some other way?'

She shrugged and said nothing.

'And what makes you suppose I'll allow it?'

'What else can you do? You can hardly throw me out. I'm Caroline's mother.'

Adrian's smile grew more pronounced as he let the silence linger. Finally, strolling away to pull the bell, he said, 'An undeniable fact. But you are overlooking one small but vital point, madam. If I can toss out my *own* mother, I will have no qualms whatsoever in evicting *you*.' And while she spluttered incoherently, 'Ah … Croft. Mrs Hayward will be requiring the carriage after all. Also her luggage and that of Miss Hayward. See to it, please.'

'Certainly, my lord.'

Mrs Hayward swung round on Caroline. 'Are you going to let him get away with this?'

Caroline sighed. 'I'm sorry, Mama – but yes. I am.'

'What? You – you *can't*!'

'Stop.' Sylvia got to her feet, her face extremely pale. 'It isn't fair to put you in this position, Caroline – nor Adrian either. And it's more than I'd ever meant to ask of you. But if Mama's only doing this because I wouldn't go home, it's easily solved. I'll l-leave.'

Everyone stared at her, then jumped when Bertrand rose with a force that sent his chair skidding backwards. Quietly but very distinctly, he said, 'No. No, Sylvie.'

She shook her head sadly. 'I have to. It's the only way to put an end to all this.'

Bertrand circumnavigated the table until he reached her side and could take her hands in his. 'No, *cherie*. It isn't. There's one other.'

Mrs Hayward started towards them saying, 'Stop that!' only to be halted by Adrian's fingers closing hard around her forearm.

'This is not what we'd intended,' continued Bertrand. 'You wanted time – and I wanted you to have it so that when … when I asked, we would both be sure that, whatever your answer was, it would be the right one.' He smiled a little ruefully. 'For myself, of course, I have been sure almost from the beginning.'

Flushing a little, Sylvia said hesitantly, 'What are you saying?'

'I think you know.' Still holding her hands, he sank down upon one knee. 'Mademoiselle Sylvie … will you grant me the very great honour of becoming my wife?'

'No,' shouted Mrs Hayward. 'Don't you *dare*, Sylvia! I forbid it!'

'Oh *do* be quiet,' muttered Lily Brassington.

'Yes,' said Madeleine and Cassie, more or less in unison. '*Do*.'

Her eyes locked with those of Bertrand, it was doubtful if Sylvia even heard them. Her fingers tightened on his and smiling tremulously back at him, she said, 'Yes. Oh yes, Bertrand. Yes, I'll marry you and yes, I'm sure … and well, just *yes*.'

He let her draw him to his feet. 'Thank you, *cherie*. You won't regret it.'

'I know I won't.'

The scattering of applause partially drowned out Mrs Hayward's howl of rage. Discovering that he was actually shaking a little, Bertrand pulled Sylvia into his arms and whispered, '*Je t'aime*, Sylvie. I love you.'

'I love you, too,' she whispered back. 'So will you please kiss me?'

'With the very greatest of pleasure, *ma belle*. And with all my heart.' And holding her even closer, his mouth found hers.

'I'm impressed,' remarked Sebastian to the room in general. 'He's got more nerve than I thought. Certainly more than *I* have. In fact, the only other gentlemen who might equal him is you, Julian.'

Julian choked over a mouthful of ham. '*Me?*'

'Yes. As I recall it, you more or less proposed to Arabella in front of a hundred or so people at Wynstanton House.'

'I didn't!'

'You most certainly did – though not in those exact words,' said Cassie severely. 'I remember it distinctly. It was wonderfully romantic!'

Throughout all of this, Mrs Hayward had (for once) been speechless with fury. Now, recovering herself, she snapped bitterly, 'You stupid, *stupid* girl. What have you done?'

'She has accepted a very proper and honourable proposal and made your own opinions redundant,' Adrian informed her calmly. 'An extremely unexpected development which is entirely your own fault, you know.'

'*My* fault? It's nothing of the sort! This is *your* doing – yours and Caro's. Why, he hasn't even got a *home* to offer her, let alone the money to support her!'

'In fact he has both. As the manager of my son's estate, he will naturally occupy Devereux House.' He shot a brief, warning glance at Bertrand. 'And as a wedding present, I shall give him a five percent share in a business of which I am part-owner. Does that satisfy you?'

Shaking her head, Mrs Hayward said, 'He's still rushing Syl into this and --'

'Oh, that's enough.' Adrian no longer sounded patient. 'They were attempting take things slowly and would have continued to do so had you not brought matters to a crisis. So any blame – if blame there is – rests squarely on your shoulders, madam. No one else's.'

Across the room, the ladies were clustering around Sylvia while the gentlemen took turns shaking Bertrand's hand. Adeline and Arabella, entering the room with Rosalind, stopped dead on the threshold, causing Rosalind to say, 'What's happening?'

'That,' said Adeline, 'is what *I'd* like to know. What have we missed?'

'I regret to say, my love,' remarked Rockliffe lazily, 'that you have missed the most entertaining breakfast I believe I have ever witnessed. One might even say that it's been better than a play. But the happy outcome is another betrothal.'

'Bertrand and Sylvia?' asked Arabella, smiling. 'How lovely.'

'That's a matter of opinion,' huffed Mrs Hayward. 'And there'll be no wedding if I have anything to do with it.'

'Which is why you won't,' said Adrian. 'You and Lavinia will return to Twickenham as planned. Sylvia will remain here with Caroline and me for ... let us say two more weeks. That should be sufficient for the happy couple to decide when and where they wish to be married and for you to come to your senses. And in the meantime – with Bertrand's permission – I shall send a formal notice to the *Morning Chronicle*.' He paused and then added, 'Yes. I believe that takes care of everything.'

* * *

Having taken an unexpectedly tearful farewell of Lavinia and gratefully leaving Caroline and Adrian to see her mother off, Sylvia sat beside Bertrand and savoured the silence. After a while, she said, 'Mr Audley was right.'

'About what?'

'About how brave you were, offering for me like that.'

Sliding an arm about her and drawing her head on to his shoulder, he said, 'It took little courage to ask. It took a great deal of it to accept that you might say no.'

'Surely you knew I wouldn't?'

'No. All I had was the *hope* that you wouldn't.' He paused and then added hesitantly, 'You can still change your mind, Sylvie.'

She swivelled round to look at him. 'Why would I do that?'

'I proposed in a roomful of people and took you completely by surprise. It wouldn't be unreasonable if --'

'Stop this minute. Yes, you asked me to marry you in front of everybody – and I *loved* you for it. No girl ever had a better proposal.'

'They didn't?'

'No. So if you think I'm going to let you off the hook now I've caught you, you're addled. I'm marrying you – and that's that.'

For a handful of seconds, Bertrand stared at her with a species of bemused shock. Then starting to laugh, he said, 'Do you know ... have you any idea of how like your mother you just sounded?'

Sylvia grinned back at him.

'Well, they say the apple doesn't fall far from the tree, don't they? So perhaps you'd better get used to it.'

'I don't think that will be a problem,' he murmured, pulling her on to his lap. 'Provided, of course, that you make a few ... allowances ... of your own.'

CHAPTER THIRTEEN

While drama was raging downstairs amongst the adults, arguments of a different kind – the ones which had made Adeline and the other ladies late for breakfast – had continued in the nursery.

John and Vanessa wanted to see – and also perhaps share – Ellie's goat. Ellie wanted them to see Daisy as well and would have been perfectly happy to share. Unfortunately, Nanny and the nursery-maids declared the stables far too cold and dirty for their small charges and were unanimous in issuing a veto which the children's mamas knew better than to contradict.

'I'm sorry, John – but if Nanny says no, then no it is,' said Rosalind gently.

'Not even for five minutes?' he asked hopefully. 'Please?'

Seeing her ladyship hesitate, Nanny said firmly, 'No, Master John. You might pick up fleas or ticks or the lord knows what.'

'Daisy hasn't got fleas,' protested Ellie indignantly. 'I helped Jemmy give her a bath.'

'And both of you ended up wetter than Daisy,' grinned Arabella. 'I imagine parasites of any kind were all drowned.'

Nanny folded her arms, sniffed and continued to look intractable.

'Want see Ellie's goat,' cajoled Vanessa for the third time. 'With Papa?'

Only too aware that Papa would give way the first time of asking, Adeline decided it might be best if he stayed out of the nursery until the wretched goat had been eclipsed by something else. She said, 'Papa is busy this morning, pet. And Nanny knows best.'

Vanessa shook her head. '*Papa* knows best.'

'Usually. He *usually* knows best. But not in the nursery. Here, we do what Nanny tells us to do.'

'Why?' asked John.

And, 'Why?' echoed Vanessa.

Adeline opened her mouth and then, unable to think of a clinching argument, said cravenly, 'Because both of your mamas say so. Now ... stop arguing and finish your breakfasts. Then, if you're good, we can play skittles in the long gallery.'

* * *

Ellie ate her porridge. She helped Vanessa play skittles but not so much that it was unfair to John. And all the time, she considered the Goat Problem.

The stables weren't *that* cold – nor were they dirty. The head groom, Mr Watson, was very fussy about how the horses were cared for and would have been insulted at the very suggestion. Moreover, Vanessa's papa had gone to see Daisy ... had even knelt in the straw and stroked her ... and he was a *duke*. Sir Julian had done the same, of course, but that didn't count because it was the sort of thing he did all the time anyway. And none of it explained why Nanny and the mothers were so dead set against a quick visit to the stables.

Ellie weighed up her chances of getting John and Vanessa to Daisy and back again without anyone being any the wiser ... and came to the conclusion that they weren't very good. Actually, they'd be lucky to get as far as the foot of the stairs before somebody stopped them.

The next thought arrived slowly. If she couldn't take the children to Daisy ... was there a way of taking Daisy to *them*? That, Ellie decided, didn't sound nearly so difficult. She'd put Daisy on a leash like Figgy and there was a side-door to the hall that hardly anyone ever used. It occurred to her that, in a house like this, there must be another staircase somewhere – a less fancy one for the servants. But since she didn't know where it was, she'd have to go up the main one that rose to a half-landing before branching out on either side towards the main reception rooms in both wings. After that, the only really tricky bit would be getting up two further flights without anyone seeing; and the best chance of *that* was when all the grown-ups were gathered for tea in the drawing-room and the footmen had finished serving. She ought to be able to count on at least five minutes of there being nobody in the hall or on the stairs. Once she got to the nursery, one of the maids would probably kick up a fuss but Nanny took a nap in the afternoons and rarely came to the nursery tea. Finally, Ellie knew she'd be in trouble later ... but that didn't matter very much since the mission would have succeeded.

Briefly, she considered enlisting the help of her brothers but decided against it. Tom would tell her not to do it. He *always* told her not to do things. As for Rob, she didn't really see that there was much he could do aside from keeping a look-out and she'd have to do that for herself anyway. Consequently, the only other thing to think about was whether or not to let John in on the secret so he'd be ready and waiting. In the end, she decided that she would. John might only be little – but he wasn't stupid.

She wandered out to the stables about half an hour before tea. Used to seeing her at odd times, the grooms took little notice. However, Daisy knew her now and danced to the front of the empty stall that was her temporary home. Ellie petted her and fed her some pieces of cooked potato while looking around her for something she could use as a tether. Finally her eye settled upon some discarded coils of stout string – the sort used for tying up heavy parcels. She picked a piece up, decided it would probably do and set about making one end into a loop that would go around Daisy's neck while the rest served as a leash. She wasn't very good at knots so she tied it twice just to be on the safe side. Then, slipping it over Daisy's head while distracting her with another piece of potato, she unlatched the stall.

Daisy bounded out … but fortunately only far enough to investigate Ellie's pockets. Ellie giggled, gave her another bit of potato and then whispered, 'You're going to meet some new friends – so be good.'

Getting across the yard and into the house was easy. Once inside the hall, however, Daisy immediately baulked and then, dragging Ellie behind her, took off in the wrong direction, her hooves clattering noisily on the stone-flagged floor. By dint of a massive effort, Ellie managed to haul her towards the stairs, hissing, 'Oh hush! If someone hears --'

But Daisy took the stairs at a gallop, two steps at a time, nearly pulling Ellie off her feet and then, reaching the half-landing seemed unable to decide on which way to go. Panting, Ellie towed her to the left and up they went to the first floor in another rush. Thankful that the carpet runner was muffling the noise, Ellie tried to pause for a moment to catch her breath before heading up the next flight. Daisy, seeing another exciting climb lying just ahead, had other ideas. For a second, she was perfectly still, poised in contemplation … and then, without any warning at all, she leapt for the stairs.

Taken by surprise and thrown off-balance, Ellie tripped and measured her length on the floor, the tether being wrenched from her fingers. She gasped, 'No! Come back!'

Too late. Daisy gained the next half-landing and shot off, onwards and upwards. Ellie, still scrambling to her feet became sickeningly aware that someone was on their way down. Realising that disaster was looming, she tried to shout a warning but all that came out was a sort of strangled groan. A startled scream pierced the air, immediately followed by the sound of falling … and Ellie had a brief, confusing glimpse of lilac silk, white petticoats and raven-dark hair as the lady they belonged to tumbled down to the half-landing, her hands wildly groping for the bannister. Then she collided with the solid oak newel ... and dropped in a crumpled heap. It was the Marchioness of Amberley.

Racing up to her, panic-stricken, Ellie started frantically chafing her hands.

'Help! *Somebody help!* Wake up, my lady – please, please wake up. I'm so sorry. I didn't mean it. Please don't be dead.' And again, desperately, '*Help!* Why doesn't --?'

Above her, the drawing-room door opened on Adrian who said, 'What's happening?' Then, taking in the situation at a glance and managing not to trip over Daisy as she shot between his legs, he hurtled down the stairs shouting, 'Amberley – Julian – I need help here. And somebody catch the blasted goat!'

Several things happened at once. From the drawing-room came a ragged chorus of shrieks and exclamations, the sound of breaking china and a loud thud accompanied by a grunt of pain. Summoned by the commotion, Croft appeared on the lower landing and called uncertainly, 'My lord?'

'Send for the doctor. And tell Mrs Holt she'll be needed in the marchioness's room.' He dropped to his knees and sought the pulse below Rosalind's jaw.

Completely distraught, sobbing and rocking from side, Ellie said, 'I'm sorry, I'm sorry. She w-won't wake up. Is she d-dead?'

'No.' He looked up to where the marquis stood, white-faced and seemingly frozen, with Julian two steps behind. 'She's unconscious – probably hit her head on something. Croft is sending for the doctor.'

Amberley nodded, struggling to banish the sickeningly vivid memory of a child in leaf-green taffeta crumpled at the roadside and thinking, *No. Not again. Please, God – not again. Not like before.* Then, breaking through his paralysis, he ran down to his wife's side and gathered her carefully into his arms. Stroking her cheek, he said unsteadily, 'Rosalind? Wake up, love.'

'She w-won't,' moaned Ellie, releasing Rosalind's hand to clutch at Julian instead. 'I d-didn't mean it – truly I didn't. Daisy got away and – and – I'm *sorry*.'

'I know.' Julian scooped her up and stepped aside. 'We'll talk about it later.'

'We have to get her upstairs,' said Adrian. 'Do you need help lifting her?'

'No.' The marquis rose slowly, Rosalind limp in his arms. Speaking – even thinking – seemed to require a huge effort. He glanced at the huddle of anxious faces lining the upper landing and said, 'Perhaps one of the ladies could help ...'

'I'll come,' said Caroline firmly. Then, realising he couldn't see his feet past Rosalind's skirts, she added, 'And don't worry about tripping over the goat. Sebastian has it.'

Amberley carried his wife up the stairs in Caroline's wake. His mind was numb and every step felt as if he was treading through a nightmare. The last time Rosalind had suffered a blow to the head she had woken up blind. What if this time was worse? What if some other damage had occurred ... to her brain, her hearing, her memory? *Don't think of it,* he told himself. *Don't even* think *of it. She'll be fine. It's not like before. She's just taken a tumble down a few stairs and banged her head. She'll wake up and she'll be fine ... she* has *to be.*

He laid her on her bed and took a couple of steps back to allow Caroline and the housekeeper access while Rosalind's maid looked on, horrified. He said helplessly, 'What can I do?'

'Help Lady Sarre turn her on her side so I can unlace her gown and stays,' replied Mrs Holt briskly. 'Move her slowly and no more than you have to. It'll be best if we remove her clothes now so the doctor can see if there's any other injury. I doubt there's anything worse than a few bruises – but better safe than sorry, I always say.'

With excruciating care, they freed Rosalind from gown, corset and petticoats. When she was reduced to her shift and stockings and covered with a warm blanket, Caroline took one look at the marquis's pallor and haunted expression and said bluntly, 'You look ill. Go downstairs and let Adrian pour you a brandy, my lord. Betsy and I will --'

'I'm not leaving her.'

'Then at least sit down. I know exactly how you feel, believe me ... but fearing the worst won't help and when Rosalind wakes up --'

'She should have started doing that by now. It's taking too long.'

'Perhaps – perhaps not. Let's wait and see what the doctor says. And in the meantime, ask for anything you need.'

Amberley gave a jerky nod and turned swiftly in response to a tap at the door, hoping it was the damned doctor.

It wasn't. It was Arabella who walked directly across to him and said, 'I'm aware that, under these circumstances, an apology is no help at all. But I wanted you to know how very sorry Julian and I are about what has happened. It never occurred to either of us that Ellie would be foolish enough to bring that wretched creature into the house – though perhaps it should have done. And however accidental the results may have been, Ellie is truly upset to have been the cause of harm coming to Rosalind.'

Somehow managing to push past the fog in his brain, he said, 'I know why she did it. Rosalind told me about this morning. Tell her ... tell Ellie she isn't to blame.'

'That is very generous of you, my lord. But I think I shall merely tell her that *you* don't blame her ... which is more than any of us could expect.' She paused, glancing at Rosalind lying pale and still on the bed. 'I'll leave you now. Perhaps it may help to know that all of us are praying for her.'

It was a further forty minutes before the doctor arrived. Amberley spent them in a chair at the bedside, his eyes never leaving his wife's face. The only colour in it was that of the bruise slowly blossoming on her left temple at the edge of her hairline. Although her lids flickered from time to time, her eyes didn't open. But her breathing was soft and regular and the pulse under his fingers remained steady ... so he tried to comfort himself with that.

Doctor Wentworth bustled in saying, 'Good afternoon, my lord. I'm told the lady fell on the stairs and hasn't yet recovered consciousness. Is that correct?'

'Yes.' Amberley swallowed hard. 'It's been over an hour.'

'That is not necessarily a bad sign.' Setting his bag aside, the doctor lifted Rosalind's wrist and checked her pulse. 'Good. Nothing wrong there. Let us discover if she has sustained any further injuries. Then, if all is well, we can consider the blow to her head.'

While he carefully examined Rosalind's wrists, shoulders and joints, he asked a few questions about her health in general, finishing with, 'Is there any possibility that she is currently with child, my lord?'

'It's a possibility, I suppose ... but not very likely. Her courses finished just over a week ago.' Amberley shoved a hand through his hair and suddenly realising what he *hadn't* yet said, blurted out, 'My wife is blind. She's been blind since she was ten years old.'

'Ah. Perhaps that explains the fall. A momentary imbalance or --'

'No. She tripped over a goat.'

Doctor Wentworth's bushy brows rose but he said merely, 'A goat. Dear me. That *is* unusual. However, the good news is that her ladyship has no injuries other than the blow to her head. Her pupils are a little dilated but not excessively so and her pulse remains steady. She will wake when her body is ready to let her. Do not attempt to hasten the process.' Stepping back from the bedside, he nodded sympathetically at the marquis. 'Your lordship's concerns are most natural – but try not to be too anxious. I don't think she will keep you waiting for very long and while she does, you might try talking to her. I shall call again in the morning but don't hesitate to summon me before then if you feel it necessary.'

Five minutes after the doctor had left, the door opened again on Rockliffe bearing a decanter of brandy and two glasses. He said, 'How is Rosalind? And how are *you*?'

'She's fine except for the blow to her head and apparently she'll wake up when she feels like it,' growled Amberley. 'As for me ... I'm half out of my mind.'

'Of course.' The duke poured two measures of brandy, held one out to his friend and, before he could refuse, said, 'Take it, Dominic. I'm not suggesting you get drunk. But just at present you look worse than Rosalind does, so you need this. Drink it.'

Amberley sighed and took an obedient swallow. 'Is the child still hysterical?'

'When last I saw her, yes. But Arabella and Julian took her to their rooms and are still with her as far as I know. As for the goat ... Sebastian succeeded in catching it before the drawing-room was *entirely* destroyed.' A faint and very rueful smile dawned. 'Your son and my daughter are loudly lamenting the fact that Adrian returned it to the stables before they had a chance to see it.'

Amberley came to his feet. 'Oh God. John! I ought to --'

'Sit down. Aside from missing the goat, John is perfectly happy. He has been told that his mama had a small accident and needs to sleep. Nicholas and Madeleine are staying with him ... and Hubert Maitland is entertaining him with conjuring tricks. There is nothing for you to do elsewhere and this is where you belong right now – so sit.'

Mumbling something indecipherable, the marquis sank back into his chair. After a moment or two, he said, 'The doctor said I should talk to her. But the only things I can think of to say aren't ... helpful.'

'That is only your opinion. And does what you say matter? You won't be holding a conversation, after all.' Rockliffe drained his glass and set it down in order to briefly squeeze his friend's shoulder. Then, sauntering to the door, he added, 'However, I fully understand that you would prefer to chat to Rosalind in private, so I will leave you for a little while. A footman has been left on duty outside the door. If she wakes or you need anything, he'll relay your orders.'

When the duke had gone, Amberley finished his own drink and, realising that the light had begun to fade, rose to light some candles. Then, sitting on the side of the bed, he took Rosalind's hand in one of his and used the other to lightly stroke her cheek. Finally he drew a long breath, tried to find his usual tone … and began to talk.

* * *

Somewhere outside the darkness that held her captive, Rosalind could hear a voice. It was a beautiful voice – low, melodic and comforting; and although she couldn't distinguish what the voice was saying, the sound of it made her feel happy and safe.

After a little while, some of the words reached her.

'Wake up, love … wake up and come back to me … I'm here, waiting for you …' And later, 'You moved your hand … clever girl … can you feel mine? Can you even hear me?'

The heavy fog inside Rosalind's head was gradually clearing. She wanted to tell him that yes, she could hear him – but it seemed too difficult so she settled for shifting her fingers in his and attempting a smile. The voice changed, becoming urgent and hopeful. 'You're starting to wake, aren't you? There's my beautiful, brave girl. Keep fighting, sweetheart. Stay with me, now … no sliding back to sleep and leaving me alone.'

Dominic? she thought, confused. *I've left you alone? But I wouldn't. Ever.*

'Why the frown, love? You're nearly there. Can you try to open your eyes for me?'

Nearly where? Open my eyes? Why?

Every pulse in her body gave a sudden, violent jolt as the thing that had been prickling at her mind came into focus; a thing that, even in her current, muddled state, she knew to be impossible. On the other side of her closed eyelids was … light.

She was abruptly fully conscious, aware … and terrified.

Light? How can that be? It can't. I must be imagining it.

But she knew she wasn't. She had lived in total darkness for nearly sixteen years, longing for the merest glimmer of light … and now, there it was. But she didn't dare believe in it. What if she opened her eyes and it wasn't really there at all? It was better to leave them closed and continue to enjoy the possibility that it might be real.

'Rosalind.' Although it was still gentle, Dominic's tone told her that he knew she was awake. 'Speak to me. Tell me how you feel.'

'I have …' She stopped to moisten her lips. 'I have an awful headache.'

'Of course you have.' Despite the crack in his voice, she heard the smile. 'Of course you have, poor love. I'll get them to send up something for it.'

She felt the bed shift as he rose, heard him cross the room and open the door.

Now, she told herself. *It has to be now.*

Harnessing all of her courage, she opened her eyes – and immediately closed them against the dazzling glare of what looked like a hundred candles. Dominic was still outside the room, talking to someone. There was time to try again. More cautiously, her heart thundering like a dozen drums, she did so. It was better this time. Still hopelessly blurred but not as startling. Red. There was a lot of red. And on the other side of the room, a big painting in a heavy gold frame. Then she heard Dominic's step and hurriedly let her lids fall.

He came back to sit on the edge of the bed and brush back a lock of hair from her cheek. He said, 'Mrs Holt will bring you a tisane. Does anything else hurt?'

'M-my elbow and one of my knees. I must have banged them on something.'

'Very likely. Do you remember what happened?'

'Yes. Ellie's goat – at least I suppose it was that – tripped me on the stairs. Why are you asking?'

'Because you've been unconscious for rather a long time. And,' he added, sounding puzzled, 'you don't seem to want to open your eyes.'

That wasn't true. She *did* want to, very much indeed. She just wasn't ready to trust what seemed to have happened to her in case it vanished as quickly as it had come … which also meant she wasn't ready to tell anyone; not even him. But if it didn't last, this was her one and only chance to see her husband's face and if she wasted it she would regret it for the rest of her life. So she turned her head to where she knew he was and very, very slowly raised her lashes.

Hazy and indistinct as it was, the sight of him caught her unprepared. Gleaming silver-gilt hair, eyes of willow-green, high sculpted cheekbones and a mobile mouth whose kisses she knew but whose smile she had yet to see. For years she'd overheard ladies describing him as the handsomest man in London … but the reality of him stopped her breath.

His expression changed, gathered a hint of anxiety. 'Rosalind? What's wrong?'

She tried to say that nothing was but she couldn't get the word out. Joy and terror were locked in an equal struggle. She dared neither move nor blink in case the precious gift was snatched away. But if it was going to be, did he not deserve to share it while it lasted? He had tried so hard to find a cure and bled, inside and in secret, because he couldn't. So if this moment was all they were to have, it surely belonged to both of them.

Keeping her eyes locked on his face, she stretched out a hand to trace his cheek and said unsteadily, 'You are so beautiful – more than I ever imagined.'

Amberley went completely still, staring back at her. Then, as if the words terrified him, he whispered, 'You can ... you can *see* me?'

'Yes.'

'Really, truly ... *see* me?'

'Not as clearly as I would like but ... yes.' She both felt and saw the shudder that went through him as he tried to take it in. Understanding that, like her, he needed something to help him believe, she said simply, 'The bed hangings are red. And over there is a big painting of a landscape with – with cows?'

And that was when he knew it was true. He dragged her into a hard embrace, burying his face in her hair while his whole body shook. Rosalind laid her hand on his nape, aware that he was weeping with mingled shock, incredulity and joy. But after a moment, she forced herself to say softly, 'It may ... Dominic, it may not last. Perhaps we shouldn't trust it yet.'

'It will last,' he replied, his voice muffled. 'God couldn't be that cruel. You've been so brave for so long ... He owes you this.' He raised his head and looked at her, his eyes blazing into hers. Then, seeming to recognise something, 'But if you're afraid of losing it before you've seen our children, I'll go and fetch them now.'

'Yes – oh yes!' Her smile dazzled him for a second before doubt muted it. 'But then the whole house will know ... and I don't think I'm ready for that. Not until we can be sure. Am I being foolish?'

'No, love. And we shall handle this however you wish.' He thought for a moment. 'However, Deb doesn't talk yet ... and John can keep a secret. Lord knows, he's kept enough of them in the past – such as the times I took him about the estate and let him romp with the tenants' children. Or the day at the lake when --' He stopped, looking slightly sheepish. 'Let's just say that I don't *always* follow nursery rules and that John keeps our occasional adventures to himself.'

The lovely amethyst eyes widened. 'You're encouraging your son to disobey Nanny?'

'Yes. A terrible father, aren't I?' He grinned unrepentantly and then rose in response to a knock at the door. 'This must be your tisane. Lie back and close your eyes.'

Mrs Holt came in carrying a tray. Setting it on a table, she said, 'Something for her ladyship's headache and wine and sandwiches for you, my lord. And Lady Sarre says I'm to tell you how happy everybody is that her ladyship is awake but that nobody will visit until you say they can. Will there be anything else I can do for you?'

'No, thank you. I believe you – and Lady Sarre – have covered everything.'

He waited until the housekeeper had gone before placing the tisane in Rosalind's hands and saying, 'Now ... if you wish it, I'll fetch the children while you drink that. But first some ground rules. You will remain as still as possible and do not even *think* of getting out of bed before tomorrow. We don't know what has restored your sight but it seems logical to assume that something has shifted back to the way it was before the carriage accident dislodged it. If that's so, it makes sense to give it time to settle. Agreed?'

'Yes.'

'Good girl.' He dropped a butterfly kiss on her brow and left the room.

Sipping the tisane and finding it less nasty than these things usually were, Rosalind looked around the room. The blurriness that had afflicted her vision when she first opened her eyes seemed to be gradually lessening and things were acquiring sharper edges. A few books lay on a table by the window and caused a starburst of optimism as she slowly began to absorb the fact that the many things which for so long had been outside her reach might be hers again.

Amberley returned, carrying Deborah and holding John's hand. He placed the baby in her lap and lifted the little boy on to the side of the bed. For a moment, gazing in wonder at the lovely children she and Dominic had made, Rosalind could scarcely breathe. John, fair-haired like his father but possessed of solemn blue eyes; and green-eyed, dark-haired Deborah, clearly destined to be a beauty one day. Tears threatened and she had to blink them away before John noticed and started to worry.

Amberley ruffled the boy's hair and said, 'Mama has a secret to tell you, John.'

The blue eyes widened. 'A secret, Mama?'

She nodded. 'A very special secret which, just for a little while, is only between you and me and Papa.'

'I know what a secret is,' said John, looking mildly offended.

'Of course you do.' Rosalind glanced briefly at Amberley, seeing the laughter in his eyes. 'They told you I'd fallen on the stairs, didn't they?'

'Because of Ellie's goat.'

'Yes. Well, afterwards I was asleep for quite a long time. But when I woke up, something strange and wonderful had happened.' She hesitated and then, deciding that simple was best, said, 'I can see again, darling. I can see you and Papa and Deborah. Isn't that splendid?'

For a very long time, the child stared at her in silence. Then a huge smile slowly dawned and he said, 'It's magic. Just like Ellie wanted.'

Epilogue

Having slept wrapped in her husband's arms, Rosalind awoke with almost perfect vision but agreed to remain in bed until after the doctor's visit.

The news caused Doctor Wentworth to shake his head in mystification.

'I must confess I've never heard of such a thing. I can only surmise that the original accident somehow dislodged the optic nerve and yesterday's mishap reversed the damage. But it is remarkable. Most remarkable. Almost miraculous, in fact. When it becomes known, physicians everywhere will want to write papers on it.'

'Lovely,' said Rosalind sardonically after he had gone. 'I'm going to be a nine-day wonder.'

'You're a life-time wonder to me,' returned her husband. 'However … if you're ready to share the glad tidings with our friends, I'll have a footman ask Adrian to get them all assembled in the drawing-room so that you only have to do it once.'

'Make sure he includes the Chalfont children. Ellie has to be there.'

'Of course. Shall we invite the goat as well?'

* * *

In the drawing-room, word that the marchioness was sufficiently recovered to come downstairs produced an atmosphere of light-hearted relief.

'It's amazing that she suffered nothing worse than a headache,' said Cassie. 'Not even a sprained ankle!'

'Amazing and lucky,' agreed Arabella. 'And thank goodness for it. Ellie did a very silly thing through the best of intentions and it went badly wrong. But it took half the night to stop her crying and convince her that Rosalind was *not* going to die – which naturally made it quite impossible to say the things one is *supposed* to say in such circumstances.'

Cassie glanced across the room to where Ellie huddled against Julian looking utterly woebegone, her eyes swollen with crying. 'She'll be better when she sees Rosalind and has a chance to apologise.'

'One can only hope.'

When the marquis and marchioness entered the room, everyone stared for a moment, silenced by the unmistakable glow of happiness on both of their faces. As usual, Rockliffe was first to react, saying languidly, 'Dear me. It appears we were all worrying needlessly. Rosalind, my love … you look positively radiant. If this is what comes of tangling with a goat, perhaps we should all try it.'

There was a scattering of laughter. But before anyone else could speak, Ellie tore herself away from Julian and ran across to throw her arms about Rosalind's waist, saying, 'I'm sorry. I'm so sorry you were hurt. It was all my fault but I didn't mean it and --'

'Hush, darling.' Rosalind sank on to the nearest chair and pulled the child into the curve of her arm. 'It was an accident, that's all. And not such a terrible one either.'

'But --'

'Ellie? Stop.' Amberley went to stand beside Rosalind's chair, his hand on her shoulder. 'My lady wife has a surprise for you … but you must sit down and be quiet.'

Ellie curled up at the marchioness's feet and leaned against her knee. Everyone else exchanged startled glances, then waited expectantly.

Rosalind's gaze travelled around the room and came to rest upon Mr Audley. A tiny smile bracketing her mouth, she said blandly, 'My goodness, Sebastian … when ladies kept telling me your hair was the colour of rubies in Burgundy wine, I didn't believe them. But it really *is*, isn't it?'

For perhaps five seconds the silence was deafening before a mixed chorus of exclamations and questions broke out. The only person who didn't join in was Rockliffe. He merely stalked across the room to drop on one knee before Rosalind and, taking both of her hands in his, raise them to his lips. Then he rose, enclosed the marquis in a brief, hard embrace and murmured, 'I won't ask how, Dominic. One doesn't question the hand of God. But I rejoice for you, my friend. You have waited a long time.'

Amberley looked back at the only man to whom he'd ever confessed his part in Rosalind's blindness, weeping as he'd done so. He said, 'She has waited longer. As for me, I still can't quite believe it. She … Rock, she just woke up and could see. I couldn't take it in. I still can't. And both of us are afraid it won't last.'

Ellie, meanwhile, was on her knees staring up at Rosalind.

'Is it true?' she asked urgently. 'Can you *really* see again?'

'Yes.' And because the child probably needed proof, added, 'You are wearing a pink dress and it suits you.'

And Ellie promptly burst into tears.

A little later, when Rosalind had explained the little that *could* be explained and Adrian was once more sending for champagne, Caroline said, 'So ... Ellie got her wish, after all – though perhaps not quite the way she'd intended.'

'She did indeed,' agreed Madeleine, smiling. *'C'est incroyable!'*

'Incredible and utterly *frustrating*,' observed Amberley. 'If I'd realised it only needed a bang on the head to restore Rosalind's sight, I'd have given her one years ago.'

This naturally caused some laughter into which Sebastian observed that it was comforting to know romance wasn't dead.

'What of the children?' asked Adeline. 'Deborah is too young to understand, of course – but does John know yet?'

Rosalind nodded. 'We told him last night but swore him to secrecy. He said it was magic. And then he asked if I'll be able to go riding with him and his papa now.'

'And will you?'

'I'll have to learn how first,' laughed Rosalind. 'But that is true of many things – dancing, for example. But there are so many wonderful things I'll be able to do now – too many to count. Playing with the children and walking *anywhere* without someone to guide me; *seeing* a new gown instead of having Phanie describe it to me.' She paused and looked up at her husband, 'But the best thing of all happened last night when I saw Dominic for the first time. That was ... well, I can't describe it.'

'*I* can,' remarked Amberley smugly. 'She was struck dumb by my manifold charms.'

'Modest as *well* as romantic,' grinned Sebastian.

'Rather like you,' retorted Cassie sweetly. 'In fact, *very* like you.'

The laughter and teasing continued until everyone held a glass. Then, calling for silence, Adrian said, 'My friends, I can't say I ever expected to need *quite* so much champagne during the course of this house-party – and can only be grateful that our cellar is able to meet the demand.'

'As are we all,' drawled Rockliffe.

'I'm sure,' agreed Adrian. 'But even as little as a fortnight ago, who could have predicted not just one but *two* betrothals? We have already toasted the happiness of Lily and Hubert ... but thanks to yesterday's alarms and anxieties, we have yet to congratulate our second happy pair. So please ... raise your glasses to Sylvia and Bertrand.'

The toast was made and drunk. Sylvia clung to Bertrand's hand and he whispered, 'It's fortunate that you're determined to keep me, isn't it?'

She shook her head at him and laughed.

'And now a unique cause for celebration that no one could *ever* have foreseen,' continued Adrian. 'Rosalind ... there isn't anyone in this house who didn't pray for Ellie to get her Christmas wish though none of us believed it would happen. That it has is a cause of rejoicing for all of us and has made this day truly memorable. However, I have one small difficulty. Do I propose a toast to you ... or to Ellie ... or to the goat?'

'Oh the goat, without question,' laughed Sebastian to a chorus of groans.

'To Rosalind first,' declared Rockliffe, firmly but not without amusement. 'And then, since it would only be fair, I believe we must also toast Ellie and Daisy.'

And so it was done. Glasses were raised to the smiling, blushing marchioness ... and then to a scarlet-faced, and suddenly shy, Ellie.

'And one final toast,' remarked Rockliffe languidly as soon as he could make himself heard. 'To mysteries, magic and miracles ... all of them inexplicable and all wholly unexpected – even by me.'

Author's Note

Over the years since **The Parfit Knight**, I have been asked many times to restore Rosalind's sight. The reason I never did so was that the story-line simply didn't belong in any of the subsequent Rockliffe books. It needed placing where it could be a shadowy thread throughout and enjoy centre-stage at the end ... hence **Midwinter Magic**.
But some of you may be groaning in disbelief.
A knock on the head cured Rosalind? Seriously? Are we supposed to believe that?
Well, yes. You are ... because it has really happened and here is the proof.

A lady from Florida, blinded in a car crash, recovered her sight after twenty years. She tripped over a loose tile in her kitchen; the tile flipped up, struck her in the back of the head and left her needing surgery. She awoke from the anaesthetic, able to see.

In New Zealand, a woman had been blind since the age of eleven thanks to a tumour pressing on her optic nerve. Thirteen years later, she knelt to kiss her guide-dog goodnight and hit her head on the coffee table. She went to bed blind ... and woke up able to see.

In both of these cases, doctors could only speculate on how this seeming 'miracle' had happened. And so it seems perfectly reasonable that Rosalind, who lost her sight due to a blow to the head, could recover it the same way.
Fact actually *is* sometimes stranger than fiction.

Stella Riley
September 2020

If you have enjoyed **Midwinter Magic** you may also enjoy other books by Stella Riley.

Roundheads & Cavaliers series (Books 1 & 2 available in audio)
The Black Madonna
Garland of Straw
The King's Falcon
Lords of Misrule

Stand-alone titles (both available in audio)
A Splendid Defiance
The Marigold Chain

Rockliffe series (all available in audio)
The Parfit Knight
The Mésalliance
The Player
The Wicked Cousin
Hazard
Cadenza

Brandon Brothers (available in audio)
A Trick of Fate

All audios are narrated by Alex Wyndham

For the latest news and a chance to chat with Stella, visit her at:

https://stellarileybooks.co.uk

Printed in Great Britain
by Amazon